TOTALLY PSYCHIC

TOTALLY PSYCHIC

BRIGID MARTIN

inkyard
PRESS

ISBN-13: 978-1-335-45374-7

Totally Psychic

Copyright © 2023 by Cake Creative LLC

In association with

For questions and comments about the quality of this book, please contact us
at CustomerService@Harlequin.com.

Inkyard Press
22 Adelaide St. West, 41st Floor
Toronto, Ontario M5H 4E3, Canada
www.InkyardPress.com

Printed in U.S.A.

For my grandma Lupe.

THE FERRER-JIMENEZ FAMILY TREE

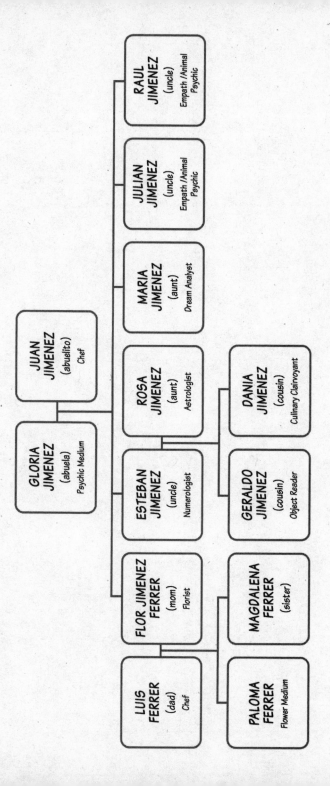

JUAN JIMENEZ (abuelito) Chef

GLORIA JIMENEZ (abuela) Psychic Medium

MARIA JIMENEZ (aunt) Dream Analyst

JULIAN JIMENEZ (uncle) Empath / Animal Psychic

RAUL JIMENEZ (uncle) Empath / Animal Psychic

ROSA JIMENEZ (aunt) Astrologist

ESTEBAN JIMENEZ (uncle) Numerologist

FLOR JIMENEZ FERRER (mom) Florist

LUIS FERRER (dad) Chef

DANIA JIMENEZ (cousin) Culinary Clairvoyant

GERALDO JIMENEZ (cousin) Object Reader

MAGDALENA FERRER (sister)

PALOMA FERRER Flower Medium

1

Abuela

My abuela, Gloria, had a gift. Not the kind that came wrapped up in a box, but the special kind that a person was born with. And for Abuela, that meant the ability to communicate with the dead. She was even pretty famous for it; in fact she was the most famous psychic in all of the world. Especially in Latin America.

So we always had more ghosts than pastelitos in our house. Which was really saying something considering the number of chefs we had in the family.

"Paloma, are we ready?" Abuela clapped her hands, commanding my attention. After lighting what had to be the hundredth candle in our kitchen, I gave her a nod.

Once a week, Abuela hosted spirit readings at our house for all of her famous friends. And tonight, I was getting to watch her channel the spirits for soap opera's own Suzanne La Luca.

Overall, a pretty normal Thursday. Right?

Abuela's revolving door of famous clientele was something I had been used to for my entire life, and Suzanne was practically family. She and Abuela went way back to when they both had TV shows on the same network in the '80s and have been super close ever since.

They sat down at the table, almost in sync with one another. Now that Abuela was semiretired, she only did at-home readings for her celebrity friends, with the exception of her legendary annual Latin American tour, and all I wanted was to see her in action on that big stage!

The dim glow from the candles embraced everything it touched, from the waxy leaves of the monstera deliciosa to the damask satin chairs that Abuela and Suzanne were currently sitting on. The kitchen looked so much more dramatic in this lighting.

I had to hand it to Abuela for her skills at setting a scene. I watched as the dancing shadows flickered across the photographs of Abuela's extensive career from her legendary and renowned TV program, *Miami Mystic*. The photos reflected a lifetime of meetings with famous people from across the globe. Even though her show had been off the air for over a decade, she still had a cult following of devoted fans, which is why she still went on her yearly tour. Even today, *Miami Mystic* remained one of the most beloved series of its kind and new viewers were constantly discovering her thanks to streaming services.

What could I say? Abuela was popular.

Abuela rolled her head back in a trance-like state as the dark mahogany grandfather clock began to chime. Her beautiful brown hands pressed against the embroidered Otomi tablecloth, a gift from one of her many admirers. I could feel the excitement well up inside me. The reading was about to begin! I studied her every move. There was still so much that I needed to learn especially since I recently discovered that I have the gift too! Talking to ghosts was kind of a family trait. Everyone used to refer to me as Abuela's mini-me because I followed her around all the time, but now that I could talk to ghosts, I was more like her than ever!

Even though I'd seen Abuela speak to spirits since I was a kid, part of me had always doubted the truth of it all, thanks to Mom. She was never really into the whole talking to ghosts thing. Then I started seeing spirits right around my twelfth birthday. July 23 to be exact. A true Leo-cusper, as Aunt Rosa liked to say. After that, any doubts still haunting me had disappeared. Like *poof*! Pure magic. I loved that I got to share this gift with Abuela. Not only could she communicate with spirits and help people receive final messages from their loved ones, but she was also the most charismatic person I'd ever met. Anyone she came in contact with instantly felt at ease in her company. She had the kind of effect on people that made them feel like they were the only person in the room, even if she was talking to a stadium of ten thousand. That was why I needed to go on tour with her, so that I could watch her connect complete strangers with their loved ones. How could I possibly expect to be like her if I didn't have a chance to study under her?

I wasn't sure how I was going to bring it up, but I was determined to ask Abuela before the end of the night if she would take me on tour with her this year. My stomach was in knots just thinking about it.

"Libranos del Mal," Abuela mumbled in Spanish under her breath. She was in full-blown concentration mode to make sure no bad spirits came through. That was the risk of doing this kind of work—potentially channeling a spirit that didn't want to leave. No one wanted to have a bad ghost following them around and causing mischief everywhere. I already had enough of that with my younger sister, Magdalena! And I wouldn't wish that on anyone. Thankfully, I'd never seen anything like that happen in the past month that Abuela had officially started letting me watch these readings.

A long pause lingered in the room as we awaited the spirit's arrival. It should be any second now.

The kitchen began to shake violently, which seemed to upset our pet cockatiel, Mango. His squawking dampened the sound of Abuela's portraits rattling against the wall. Within moments, everything was still again and Mango was back to his usual quiet self. The hairs on the back of my neck stood at attention as the hot Miami air was replaced with a chill that made it feel like we had walked into the refrigerated section of a grocery store. I burrowed deeper into my sweater. Abuela and I always wore them for this very reason.

The portal to the spirit world was now open.

We had a ghost in our midst.

A lanky translucent spirit appeared across the table. A lime-green feather collar framed her gaunt face. If I had to guess, I would say she was around the same age as Abuela. The spirit's glamorous hairdo billowed out on the sides and tapered into a neat bun at the top in a way that felt old fashioned. I'd never seen that kind of style before. Even her salmon-colored frilly gown with puffy sleeves mirrored the shape of her hair. Something about her appearance made me think of a flamingo...but not the cute kind.

I wouldn't be caught dead in an outfit like that.

Most people didn't realize that in the afterlife, you get stuck wearing whatever you died in. So unfortunately there would be no costume change for this spirit any-time soon. I couldn't imagine what she could have been doing to end up in *that*.

"Suzanne, a visitor has come through for you," Abuela enunciated in her *Miami Mystic* TV voice that she reserved especially for readings. "She appears to be a tall woman with a wonderful sense of fashion."

I stifled a laugh. She had to be joking.

"That could be any number of people in my family." Suzanne adjusted her long floral nightgown and lovingly touched the silk turban covering her hair. "We are a well-dressed bunch."

That was definitely true of Suzanne—she was every bit as fabulous in person as she was on television. Right now, she may have looked like a glamorous pajama queen, but she was the star of my favorite Spanish telenovela, *Everybody's Cousin*, where the main character finds out she's related to everyone else on the show. Mom and I used to watch it every week until the series finally ended after thirty-two seasons. Basically, Suzanne was a big deal.

I waited for the spirit to say something, but there was nothing but silence. Crossing over from the spirit world took a lot of energy, and sometimes spirits didn't have enough left to speak. In those instances, they had to resort to visual cues to get their messages across.

The spirit that came through for Suzanne started dancing for a few moments, then fell to the ground. She did this over and over again with the same shocked expression on her face.

This was going to be a test of Abuela's charade skills. Mine too. I watched carefully, hoping for a clue that would indicate what she was trying to say, but Abuela concentrated her attention on an object on the table that looked like a compact mirror. Why would Abuela be looking at that instead of the spirit?

The spirit pressed her hand against her chest as she fell once more in the middle of our kitchen.

"I see that the spirit is touching her neck to indicate that there was a necklace there." Abuela twisted the sizable turquoise beads around her own neck. "Is there a piece of jewelry that holds any important significance to you or any of your relations?"

"Yes! Yes!" Suzanne beamed. "When I was eighteen and about to go on my first audition for *Everybody's Cousin*, my aunt gave me this necklace as a good luck charm. She was an actress at one of the theatres in New York and always said there wasn't a role she didn't get while she was wearing it. This necklace gave me the confidence I needed for the audition that truly catapulted my whole career!"

The candlelight illuminated Suzanne's giant green pendant necklace perfectly. Suzanne mimed the same action as the spirit without realizing it as she touched the stone she was currently wearing. Abuela was also a fan of over-sized jewelry, but I could tell that this necklace was extra-special to Suzanne.

"What a lovely story, Suzanne. Your aunt wants you to

know that she is very proud of you and it means so much to her that you are wearing it today." Abuela looked back down at the table.

The spirit nodded.

"I never take it off!" Suzanne dabbed happy tears from her cheeks. "Did she say anything else about my acting career? Any big auditions coming up?"

"I thought you were supposed to be filming a new movie!" I gasped and then immediately covered my mouth. Abuela didn't like to be interrupted.

"That got canned, darling. You can't believe everything the tabloids tell you." Suzanne pretended to brush something off her sleeve. She looked pallid, like she lost all the color in her face.

I had clearly struck a nerve.

Abuela didn't even turn her head to look in my direction. Either she was concentrating superhard on something or she was annoyed.

Suddenly, white and yellow flowers swirled around Suzanne's aunt in an elegant dance of floral choreography. A flower premonition!

My ability to see ghosts wasn't the only thing I was good at. It didn't take long after getting my powers to realize that flowers were kind of my specialty. As a flower medium, sometimes bursts of blossoms showed up out of nowhere, which could get a little distracting. Abuela said I needed to pay close attention whenever I saw one because every flower has a unique meaning, and those meanings could help me to predict future events. Being part of a family of psychic mediums had a way of proving that being normal was overrated and that sometimes, it was the little things setting us apart that made the biggest impact.

I sat up straight and concentrated on each of the flowers that materialized around Suzanne's aunt. The small white ones were…baby's breath? No! Hemlock! The symbol for death! And that meant the yellow must be rue, the symbol of regret.

"Your aunt's messages are coming in a little fuzzy, sorry to say." Abuela took a sip of her tea. "But one message I can relay is that it wouldn't hurt to exercise a little caution the next time you're on set."

"Oh that aunt of mine, still such a worrywart even in death. The only thing I need to be careful of is the bad coffee on set." Suzanne tucked her used tissue into her sleeve.

There was a long pause as Abuela stared at the spirit.

Suzanne's aunt mimed the action of pulling back a curtain and pushing someone to the ground. I tried connecting the dots between my prediction and the movements the spirit was doing.

Did she push someone? Did she witness someone else getting pushed? Was Suzanne in danger of getting seriously hurt? Whatever it was, she was definitely trying to communicate some sort of…stage accident.

That's what my flower premonitions were trying to tell me! Suzanne was in danger! Why wasn't Abuela telling her that? If Suzanne was at risk of getting injured, she needed to hear it, or else she could get seriously hurt!

The spirit threw her hands in the air, frustrated that we weren't relaying her message. Now was my time to shine and prove to Abuela what I was capable of. Latin American tour here I come!

"There's going to be a stage accident!" I shouted proudly from the corner of the room where I had been hiding amongst the houseplants. I was already giving myself an imaginary pat on the back for getting it right.

Abuela's eyes went wide as she turned to look at me. That got her attention, but I could tell it was *not* in a good way. Abuela scrunched her face as if to say "cállate la boca." I wanted to melt into the floor.

An awkward silence stretched between us that felt like an eternity. With each second that passed by, doubt began to creep up from the pit of my stomach. Maybe I could talk my way out of Abuela's frustration.

"To be honest, it's really hard to tell what the message is. The stage accident could have even happened in the past," I said, and a flash of anxiety hit me like a fresh sunburn as I realized Abuela's expression remained unchanged. All I wanted right now was to disappear. Maybe even turn into a spirit myself.

"Stage accident?" Suzanne La Luca tilted her head. "No darling, my aunt was never in a stage accident, and like I said, I don't act in the theatre."

I looked from the spirit to Abuela, hoping for some backup.

"That's right, Suzanne. There was no accident." Abuela let out a long breathy sigh and pinched the bridge of her nose. "Paloma only started to see spirits a little over a month ago. She's got a bright future ahead of her, but she needs to work on interpreting messages. It's very easy to get things mixed up when you're first starting out. With more practice, she will get there!" Abuela flashed her signature veneered smile before blowing out the candles directly in front of her. "Why don't we call this a night, Suzanne? We can pick up again where we left off in our session next week."

As Abuela got up from the table, the room shook violently and the lights flickered back to their full brightness. Suzanne's aunt vanished with a scowl on her face. Major ghost stink eye in my direction.

Within moments, the room's temperature went back to normal, Miami's usual eighty degrees breezing through the open windows. And just like that, the reading was over.

"But…" The word barely slipped out of my mouth.

The look on Abuela's face told me that I shouldn't continue. Turned out Abuela stink eye was even worse than ghost stink eye. Now that Suzanne's aunt was gone, I felt like I lost my chance to prove to Abuela that I could help with her readings. So much for being her psychic sidekick!

"Always a pleasure to see you, my dear friend." Suzanne waved as she walked toward the back door. "And congratulations to you, Paloma, for following in your grandma's footsteps! Must be very exciting for you."

"Uh-huh." I nodded as I slinked deeper into the corner where the parlor palms and the rest of the houseplants lived. At least I felt safe amongst the foliage where I couldn't do any more damage. Abuela escorted her friend to the atrium and out the front gate. I watched her long robe graze the floor behind her as she left. She looked as if she were gliding on air instead of travertine.

After Abuela returned to the kitchen, she pulled the satin chair to the table and gestured for me to come sit beside her. I felt frozen in place with my back pressed up against the pineapple wallpaper, my legs refusing to move. They must have sensed I was in trouble.

Big trouble.

2

Goodbyes

Abuela was rarely mad at me, but she had a hidden temper that she only reserved for special occasions—or for Mom. But I had a feeling that tonight her anger was going to be pointed in my direction. She seemed pretty upset after I interrupted her reading.

"I think you and I need to have a chat about what just happened." Abuela's tone sounded suspiciously nice. Too nice.

She picked up the teapot which had fallen over during the reading and returned it to its upright position.

"Tea?" she asked. Her eyebrows were raised.

This had to be a trick question. I looked at her skeptically, trying to pick up on any visual cue that this might be a trap.

"Are you mad at me for interrupting you?" I wasn't going to move from my protected spot until I got some verbal confirmation that I wasn't in trouble.

"No, not at all," Abuela's tone ascended. "You know I always welcome your input. Mistakes are bound to happen."

Verbal confirmation of my not being in trouble, received! I walked over to sit next to her at the kitchen table.

"But it wasn't a mistake, or at least it wasn't all a mistake," I said. "The spirit mimed the actions of pulling a curtain and pushing someone, which I know you could see! What else could that possibly mean besides an accident?"

There had to be something the spirit was trying to say. Why else would Suzanne's aunt keep repeating the same thing over and over again if it wasn't important?

"Oh, it was a mistake, my dear. But for different reasons than you think." Abuela poured herself another cup of herbal tea, took a sip and shifted her chair closer to mine. "Suzanne's aunt was communicating that *she* had caused a stage accident, injuring another actress in her youth. That angry spirit of the actress she injured is looking to get her revenge on Suzanne. But it's not our job as mediums to alter the future. That kind of information might cause Suzanne to be too afraid to live her life if she's constantly worrying that something bad is about to happen."

"So you didn't tell Suzanne the message about the stage accident on purpose, even if something bad is actually about to happen?" Clearly Abuela had gotten messages from the spirit that I missed, but it felt wrong not to say anything. Shouldn't Suzanne have a right to know that she was going to be the victim of a vengeful ghost? Her aunt *wanted* to warn her. I didn't care what the rules were. If we got a message, we should deliver it!

"That is precisely right," Abuela said. "Our job is to help make the grieving process a little easier for those of us left on Earth. You can understand that, can't you, mi nieta?"

I wasn't sure I liked this rule, but I was too afraid to look at the disappointed expression on Abuela's face.

"I'm never going to be as good as you, am I?" I stared at my shoes.

"You are already great, my darling. And thankfully there was no harm done." Abuela put her hand on my knee. She always knew the right thing to say to make me feel better.

"Does this mean I can go on tour with you?" I asked.

Maybe now wasn't the best time to bring it up, but I

didn't know when the next time would be that I would get the chance.

"Darling." Abuela paused. "You know your mother would never allow that. Besides, you still need to practice getting a handle on your powers and you'll have so much going on at your new school that you won't even miss being on tour. I hear the spirits in California are much chattier! You can even start doing your own readings!"

Ugh. Why did she have to bring that up? I'd been trying to ignore the move for weeks and I just blew my last chance for escape. I'd have to come up with another way to prove to Abuela that she should take me with her. I wasn't ready to give up just yet. Her tour wasn't until the first week of December, so there was still plenty of time to show her that I was ready.

"I can't believe Mom is moving us across the country because I started getting spirit messages over the summer!" I slinked deeper into the chair. "It isn't fair. She's literally ruining my life. What am I supposed to do without my friends? What am I supposed to do without you?"

Mom always hated the fact that everyone in our house had psychic abilities, and now that I got my powers, we suddenly ended up moving. What other reason could there be for us to move other than Mom not wanting me to practice summoning ghosts with Abuela? It's the only explanation that made sense.

"You know I'd never let you move if something bad was going to happen. I am a psychic after all." Abuela put her soft hand on top of mine. Her brown eyes twinkled like a flame. "And remember, I'm only one phone call away if you ever need to talk."

One phone call away?

It felt like I was being dumped by my own grandma.

Not to doubt Abuela's psychic powers or anything, but what if she was wrong? California was pretty far away. Maybe her psychic powers wouldn't reach!

My anxiety thought bubble burst at the sound of knocking on the back door. It was my best friends, Jasmin Lord and Keisha Taylor!

"Abre la puerta," Abuela called out. We had an open door policy in this house.

"Hey, Paloma! Hey, Mrs. Jimenez!" Keisha shouted through the glass.

"Hope we're not bothering you guys!" Jasmin let herself inside. "Just wanted to say goodbye before the big move."

"Very sweet of you girls," Abuela said. "I'll leave you to it."

I walked with them into the atrium where we could be alone. Everything around us glowed from the strings of fairy lights wrapped around each of the palm trees that encircled the space as the fountain gurgled in the background. Lights danced across the trickling water.

"We know it's kinda late and you have that early flight tomorrow." Jasmin's voice cracked. Her purple eyeliner was smudged around her lower lids like she had been crying. "But we couldn't let you go without saying goodbye! We practically had to elbow our way past the paparazzi at your front door to get here."

Paparazzi were always outside on Thursdays for the celebrity readings. That was part of the reason why Mom wasn't a fan of the fame attached to Abuela's work as a medium. She liked her privacy. If Mom had her way, this would be my last reading ever, since we were moving tomorrow. She wasn't exactly happy I was helping Abuela instead of finishing packing.

"I can't believe you came!" I hugged them both. "I hope this is a kidnapping scheme and you have some kind of elaborate plan to rescue me from moving across the country."

"Oh my gosh, why would we stop you?" Keisha pulled

away from the hug, her deep brown skin glistened in the lamplight. "We wish we could come with you!"

"Yeah, Paloma, this is really cool," Jasmin said as she fussed with her electric-blue hair. She was always messing around with box dyes. "You're going to love it out there, trust me! My sister went to LA once with her college friends and told us she wasn't ever coming back. My mom had to threaten to cut off her credit cards until she booked her flight home. Bet you won't want to come back once you're out there either!"

"Totally," Keisha said. "Plus, Jasmin and I were already looking at tickets for winter break. So, you're not getting rid of us that easily."

"You're right. The kidnapping plan would have never worked anyway," I said as I looked up at the sky, wishing that I wasn't about to leave everything I'd ever known behind. There was too much light pollution to see anything more than a few stars. "My mom would have caught on the second I was gone. She has a sixth sense for that sort of thing. Guess I should at least try to give LA a chance."

"That's the spirit! Pun intended!" Jasmin said. "Though we'll miss bailing you out, like that time Mr. Cooper almost sent you to the principal's office for 'making a mockery of science' with your psychic reading before you even had any powers. Like, what were you thinking?!"

"Yeah, that was pretty rough to watch. You were so lucky Jasmin yelled 'April fools!'" Keisha nudged my arm.

Abuela's atrium was filled with hand-carved marble statues of famous mediums and astrologers throughout history, from Mina Crandon to Miss Cleo. I knew them all by heart.

"Remember the time we were all convinced that we heard something coming from the Fox sisters fountain?" I leaned against a garden statue of Walter Mercado.

"And then it turned out to be Magdalena hiding behind a nearby azalea bush booing us." Keisha laughed. "It was our favorite spot ever since."

"I'm really going to miss you both so much." I could feel my eyes getting mistier by the second.

"We'd be mad if you didn't." Jasmin plucked a leaf off one of the ferns and held it against her upper lip like a mustache in an attempt to lighten the mood. "Promise you'll call as soon as you're unpacked. We want to know everything."

"Promise." I hugged them both goodbye.

I didn't want to let go.

3

The Book of Flowers

I walked back inside and practically flopped my entire body over my steamy mug of chamomile that Abuela left steeping on the table. I was still in the denial phase about this move.

"I always liked those two," she said as she pulled out an old hat box from the pantry. "It's important to have good friends in your life. And speaking of important things, tengo algo bien especial para ti."

"You have something special for me?" I forced myself out of a ninety-degree angle as she placed the box on the table in front of me.

"I originally intended this to be a Christmas gift, but I

figured you'd need a little cheering up before your trip."
She put her hand on top of the lid. "But before you open
it, I'd feel a lot better, especially after this evening's incident, if you'd recite the cardinal rules of mediumship."

I should have known there would be a catch.

There were five rules that every medium needed to
know. Abuela had been reciting them to me basically since
I was born, and yet I still had somehow managed to break
them tonight. Oops!

"Number One." I cleared my throat, sitting a little
straighter. "Never try to force contact with the spirits."

Abuela always stressed this as the most important
rule. Forcing a connection with a spirit could accidentally
open a portal for negative energies to come through. This
meant no Ouija boards, no ghost tours, and no haunted
house visits. Basically, I was no fun to be around during
Halloween time.

"Number Two. Never ever talk to evil spirits."

So, if you broke rule number one or if you accidentally
summoned an evil spirit, it was important not to talk to
them. Otherwise, they'd follow you literally everywhere.

Uncle Esteban accidentally summoned an evil spirit
while he was teaching at the University of Miami. Abuela

wouldn't let him come back to the house until he figured out a way to get rid of it. He had to stay in a motel
for almost a month until he realized the spirit hated the
Ghostbuster movies. Turned out, all of those movies had
the ability to get rid of any unwanted spirits, specters, or
ghosts just by playing them! Luckily for Uncle Esteban,
Ghostbusters had a way of really living up to its name if
you'd let it.

"Number Three. Never ask spirits how they died."

Oddly enough, talk of death was a very sensitive sub-
ject for the dead. We couldn't bring up the topic unless
they wanted to share. Which they rarely did.

"Number Four. Don't repeat everything a spirit tells
you."

Aka the rule I messed up today. Technically, we weren't
supposed to repeat messages from the spirits that might
be upsetting for the person receiving the reading to hear.
But to be totally honest, I still didn't agree with this one.

"Number Five. Readings should be healing, not hurtful."

This one was sort of related to number four. We needed
to be sensitive to the fact that most people usually came
to us so that they could hear from their loved ones and try

to process their own grief, so it was important to be sure to relay messages that helped with the healing process.

"Asi es, mi vida. I'm glad that you remember all the rules." Abuela applauded.

Of course I knew the rules! She really needed to give me more credit.

"Now it's just a matter of putting them into practice." She placed the box on my lap and opened the lid. The stale perfume of long-forgotten tobacco lingered in the air. "These items will ensure that all of your readings are a success."

Everything inside the box was neatly packed in a folded white cloth with hand-embroidered flowers, similar to the one that was currently on the kitchen table. She gingerly unwrapped each bundle to reveal several candles, a compact mirror, a notebook, and something called *The Book of Flowers*.

"I've given boxes just like this one to each of my children and grandchildren once they received their psychic abilities. They were all right around the same age as you are now, and I imagine I will be giving another box to your sister when the time comes." She plucked the compact mirror off the table and held it between her hands.

"Each of the items in here was chosen specifically for you, and I want to take a moment to go over how you can use them as you begin your psychic journey. Let's start with the spirit mirror, shall we?"

"Spirit mirror?" My eyes widened. She had my full attention.

Abuela held out the gold compact engraved with my initials. The outer edges were embossed with an intricate swirl. She pressed a small button on the outer rim that made a faint clicking sound as it sprang open. I stared at it blankly, unable to figure out what I was looking at. On the outside, it looked like a fancy compact mirror, like the kind you'd see at the cosmetics counter at the mall. But inside, all that stared back at me was a shiny black surface in the place of where my reflection was supposed to be. Something told me this definitely wasn't store-bought. This was special.

"As you can see, this is not an ordinary mirror." Abuela traced her long fingernail gently across the smooth surface. "What you're looking at is obsidian, a special kind of stone. These mirrors are specifically designed to help mediums like us communicate with spirits who don't have enough energy to speak after they cross over from the spirit world. Like what happened with Suzanne's aunt during the reading today. This device really comes in handy in a pinch."

That explained how Abuela was able to pick up on what Suzanne's aunt was communicating earlier. I was wondering what she had been looking at on the table. It was the spirit mirror!

"I didn't know we got to use accessories!" My eyes were transfixed on the smooth black stone, mesmerized. "How does it work?"

There was nothing about it that seemed magical.

"Think of it like your phone line to the other side. The messages can be sent back and forth from either the spirit or a fellow medium, and their words will become transcribed on the obsidian."

"Abuela, if it's like a phone, you know I can literally just text you, right?" I picked up the mirror again and stared deeply into it. "I mean, the whole magic mirror spirit interpretation part of it seems supercool and useful and all, but I feel like this is way more complicated than texting. There aren't even buttons!"

"It is so much better than text messages, darling!" Abuela pulled out a nearly identical but slightly more tarnished silver compact mirror from her pocket. She whispered into it and closed the compact with a snap. The mirror that Abuela had given me began to vibrate and glow in the palm of my hands…kind of like a phone. The obsidian glass inside read: *Hola, Paloma, It's me! Abuela!* The font was curled in a familiar way at the ends like it had been written in her own handwriting.

Okay, fine. This was cooler than texting.

I whispered into my mirror and waited for Abuela's compact to glow. I could see my own messy handwriting come through on her device. It read: *Am I doing this right?*

This was going to be fun. Also, I really needed to work on my penmanship after seeing my chicken scratch scroll across Abuela's mirror.

Abuela reached for another set of items on the table.

"This may not look very exciting, but the most important tool in a medium's arsenal is a set of blessed candles." Abuela laid them flat in her hands. "These are especially important because they keep us protected from unwanted guests. We need to do everything in our power to keep the negative energies and bad spirits at bay. These particular candles I am giving to you were blessed by my friend Father Rick over at Saint Francis de Sales. Even though he absolutely disagrees with what I do, which is something he has in common with your mother, he does support the idea of me being protected from evil entities, which I appreciate. Plus, if he didn't give me these, it would make our weekly card night in the parish rectory very uncomfortable. Be sure you light them before any readings you end up doing."

I carefully put the candles back into the box. I did not want to come face-to-face with any bad entities.

"And next." Abuela held *The Book of Flowers*. Its golden lettering gleamed against the dark purple leather. "As you know, all mediums have their specialties, and I think it's so wonderful that your psychic gift has manifested as visions of flowers. Especially since you've spent so much time helping out in your mother's flower shop. This book will tell you all you need to know about interpreting the different types of flowers."

Abuela pulled out one last object from the box. A marbled notebook. I wondered what kind of hidden magic was tucked away in the pages.

"This is for you to write down any visions you have so that you don't forget about anything that comes to you. All premonitions are important," she said.

I paused, waiting for her to say more, but nothing came. Huh, I guess she saved the most normal gift for last. Not the order I would have chosen, but who am I to look a hat box in the mouth.

I wasn't sure if I would have enough premonitions to fill up a notebook, but I was excited to start practicing.

"Thank you, Abuela," I wrapped my arms around her. My cheeks still hurt from smiling. I couldn't wait to try these out!

4

A Family Trait

I learned pretty early on that the ability to communicate with the dead and see the future was sort of a family trait. Well, with the exception of Mom. For whatever reason, the gift sort of skipped over her and I was pretty sure it explained why she was such a grouch all the time. Mom was also the only one in the family against the whole talking to ghosts thing, so she was super upset when my psychic powers started to show up.

Besides Mom, all of my other relatives were mediums, just like me and Abuela. And like my flower premonitions, each of my relatives had different psychic abilities that was unique only to them. It tended to get a little chaotic with all of us under one roof, but I wouldn't have it any other way.

Uncle Esteban had the ability to use numbers to predict future events, and could even tell what someone's personality was! At first he just thought he was super good at math growing up, but it turned out his gift was numerology. I still didn't fully understand how it worked, but his predictions were usually spot-on. Aunt Rosa was a typical astrologist, which meant she was always looking to the sky for answers. She especially loved talking about how the stars were going to impact our lives. On most days she was fine to be around but we usually tried to stay clear of her when Mercury was in retrograde since she always seemed to get extra stressed-out during that time. Aunt Maria, my self-proclaimed "cool aunt," lived in the basement due to her nocturnal schedule as a professional dream analyst and life coach. She was always getting calls from clients in the middle of the night, but she never seemed too bothered about it. She constantly mumbled to me and Magdalena about the importance of tracking our dreams, though I couldn't remember the last time I actually used a dream journal. Then there was Uncle Raul and Uncle Julian, the twins. Both my uncles were the unique combination of being empaths and animal psychics. Because of that, they were always getting mixed up in other people's business and were constantly bringing home new pets like our cockatiel, Mango. I hadn't seen them since they flew to Texas a few weeks ago to help a friend find a lost ferret.

As for me, I was a flower medium, which meant I had the inconvenient trait of seeing flowers popping out all over the place when I least expected it. Abuela said my gift was pretty rare and that I was the first one in the family to have this gift since the 1800s or something. Seeing random flowers floating around people's heads could be distracting sometimes, but Abuela said if I kept practicing then I'd be able to control my abilities and make predictions whenever I felt like it!

I first started getting my flower premonitions last spring while helping out at Mom's flower shop, Flor's Flowers. Mom thought I had a knack for picking the right flower for the right occasion, but Abuela said it was a sign of my intuitive awakening. I was pretty sure that Mom got upset because flowers were kind of *our* thing, and once I had psychic flower powers, she realized that this was something that connected me with Abuela even more.

The premonitions started out small at first. I remembered there was a couple that came into Mom's store, and I just *knew* they were getting married. I could see swirls of roses dance around their heads which could only mean one thing, true love. It was so magical. But when I asked when the big day was, it was as if all the blood drained from the guy's face. Apparently, he'd been planning to propose to his girlfriend that night and I sort of spoiled the whole thing.

So embarrassing.

Mom didn't let me help with the customers for weeks after that. I was officially sentenced to trimming thorns off the roses in the back room.

Other than that, helping out at Mom's shop was pretty great. I was actually going to miss sweeping the fallen petals off the black-and-white-checkered floor at the end of the night. The comforting aroma felt like a weighted blanket. Plus, my flower identification skills had improved a ton.

I thumbed through the thin tattered pages of *The Book of Flowers* and noticed several different handwritings scribbled in the margins.

"What are these?" I asked as I pointed to the faded lettering.

"Ah." Abuela held the book closer to her face so she could see better. "These are notes from your ancestors who had this book long before you. Other flower mediums like yourself, who passed down their wisdom for the next flower medium in the family. As you learn more about your gift, you will be able to do the same and share your wisdom in these pages too."

I held the book close to my chest. I wanted to learn everything I could from it.

The deep hollow clang of the grandfather clock echoed throughout the room.

"Don't you think it's time for bed, Paloma?" Mom called out from the stairwell. Her voice piercing through the chimes.

Even though it was 11:00 p.m. on the dot, I wasn't ready to go upstairs yet. I needed to soak up as much time with Abuela as possible before we had to catch our flight to California in the morning.

"Paloma!" Mom shouted again.

I didn't respond. All things silent treatment for her ever since she sprang this move on us last month.

"Paloma, mi amorita, you can't go on ignoring your mom forever." Abuela put her arm around me. "Sometimes we have to do the things we don't want to in order to make us stronger."

I rolled my eyes. Just let me be *weak*, Abuela.

Mom's footsteps creaked further down the stairs. I could feel my chest tighten as she got closer. I didn't want this to be real. The thought of leaving this house and everyone I knew behind made my stomach churn in the kind of way that might feel like you're hungry but instead is just the empty feeling of dread scrambling around in the middle of your body. My eyes were so heavy from the weight of the emotions I had been trying to hold back all night. I tilted my head back to stop the tears, but it was no use. Hot wet globs trickled down the sides of my face. I squeezed my eyes tight, then felt Mom's arms wrap around me.

"My little Paloma." Mom held me to her heart. "You know I love you with every piece of me. But I think a little distance from this celebrity life will be good for you. Aren't you tired of living in the shadow of your grandma? I know I am. Plus, I don't want you ending up on some reality TV show like Dania and Geraldo."

My cousins had all the fun.

That was Mom's problem with Abuela. She just wanted to have a quiet, simple life. But every time we left the house, people would stop us to ask about the great Gloria Jimenez and if they could get squeezed into her legendary waitlist for an appointment. I loved every second of it. My ultimate dream was to one day be so famous that I couldn't leave the house without someone recognizing me.

Over the years, Abuela had done so much good by using her gift of mediumship. Her work helped people navigate their future by connecting them with their past, and I couldn't wait to be just like her someday. But Mom just didn't get it. She thought people needed to pick their own path and live in the moment.

"Your mom's right," Abuela said. "If you want to become a great medium, you're going to have to make a name for yourself like I did when I was your age, and I think this move will help you do just that."

"Isn't there something else you want to add?" Mom cleared her throat and glared at Abuela. I got the sense that this was not the first time they'd had this talk.

What was Mom's deal with not wanting me talking to ghosts anyway? Abuela literally talked to ghosts all the time. It was her actual job. Shouldn't Mom want me to have a realistic career goal? Ugh! I was almost positive she picked California just because it was on the complete opposite side of the country from Abuela. There was no other reason I could think of for why we had to move. We didn't even know anyone out there!

Abuela let out a long sigh.

"Right, of course. Please make sure to focus on your grades and your homework and church choir and all of those things too, Paloma. But more importantly," she said with a defiant glance at Mom, "think of all the new spirits you will meet and the new audience of people you'll be able to do readings for!"

"Mom! She's focusing on school. Not playing around and talking to ghosts." Mom's strained tone and the bulging vein in her neck meant she was ready for battle.

The hug was over. All that understanding...*poof*! Gone!

"Well, why not both?" Abuela rose from the table, and in the process nearly knocked over a taxidermy pheasant on the wall.

They started to squabble. Even Mango the cockatiel chimed in. But this was nothing new. Mom and Abuela argued over anything there was to argue about. TV shows, wallpaper choices, even which laundry detergent brands to buy. Whatever it was, they disagreed and the whole house had to hear about it.

"Whoa, whoa, whoa, what is going on?" Dad called out as he entered the kitchen. "Flor, honey. It's our last night here. Can we not do this?"

"Are you implying I started this, Luis? Because we both know I didn't," Mom said.

Dad, the usually really patient one, looked exhausted. "I'm just begging for one night of no arguing. This is how you want to say goodbye to your family?"

A loud snore followed by grumbling came from the chair in the living room. I had almost forgotten that Abuelito was still down here.

"What's going on in there?" Abuelito shouted. "Did the Marlins lose again?"

"Yes, but that's not what they're arguing about!" I shouted back.

Poor Abuelito, always yelling because he was hard of hearing. He was currently reclined in his favorite saddle suede chair in the living room. It was the only piece of furniture in the house that was off-limits to everyone else.

"Hey, why does Paloma get to stay up?" Magdalena, my nine-year-old sister, stomped her way into the kitchen wearing a unicorn onesie. Her light brown hair was jumbled in knots.

"Magdalena, please go back to bed. We have a long day tomorrow." Dad tried to steer my sister back up the stairs, but it was too late. She ran over to the kitchen table and grabbed my new spirit mirror.

"Hey!" I said. "Give that back!"

Magdalena darted around all of Abuela's collectibles and antique furniture from her world travels. She dashed into the living room, jumping over Abuelito, who'd fallen back asleep in his recliner, and knocked over one of Abuela's many museum-like knickknacks in the process.

The crash boomed through the house. Everyone got quiet.

I scoffed, both annoyed and impressed by her jumping skills.

"What's going on down there?" I heard my tío shout. Uncle Esteban and Aunt Rosa rushed downstairs.

Just another typical Thursday night in the Jimenez-Ferrer household.

Chaos.

Part of me felt a little sad that this might be the last big family fight under one roof.

My whole family, including my aunts and uncles, had lived together in the same house on Ocean Drive for as long as I could remember. As far as I was concerned, Miami was the best place in the world to be. Warm weather, sandy beaches, and palm trees everywhere. Plus, we had great neighbors. Abuela told me once that she had wanted to move as close as possible to the former Versace Mansion just so she could get fashion tips from his ghost. These days, all they did was gossip about the latest trends or argue over whether or not Abuela was wearing too many accessories. Which of course was always.

"What's with all this commotion?" Aunt Maria asked as she looked back and forth between Mom and Abuela. Her puffy black hair was pulled back off her face with a vibrant pink handkerchief that was tied in a knot on top of her head. She had just come inside from her nightly mindfulness stroll in the garden.

"Paloma did it!" Magdalena said.

As if! She was always quick to throw me under the bus for things I didn't do.

"Not true!" I grabbed the spirit mirror out of my sister's hand while she wasn't looking.

"Paloma, I have had enough of this acting out," Mom yelled from the other room.

"Flor," Aunt Rosa said. "Is everything okay?"

50

"No, everything is not okay. I don't know how you put up with living here," Mom scolded her siblings. "This is not the kind of lifestyle I want my children growing up around."

"It's what *we* grew up around," Uncle Esteban said. "And we turned out fine."

I could tell that he was smiling beneath his dark bushy mustache.

"Debatable," Mom said.

"I don't think this is the kind of conversation we want to be having in front of the children, dear." Dad's voice cracked. He was looking paler than usual. Fighting always stressed him out.

"That reminds me." Aunt Rosa looked over at me and my sister, who was currently doing handstands against the wall. "I need everyone to stop what you're doing and gather in the kitchen."

Mom rolled her eyes, but we all did as we were asked and migrated into the other room.

"We all know there has been some tension this evening. Plus lots of arguments over these at-home readings." Aunt Rosa made sure her gaze lingered on Mom and Abuela. Her brown cheeks were now flushed from frustration. "But

this is our last night together and I want it to be memo-
rable and special for the girls."

"Too late for that!" Uncle Esteban said.

"With the star Sirius rising, we are reminded of our pas-
sions and resentments but also of our faithfulness and
family." Aunt Rosa took an amethyst pendant necklace out
of her pocket and handed it to me gingerly. She then took
off her amethyst beaded bracelet and gave it to my sister.

I admired the light purple rock with its smooth edges
wrapped in silver. It reminded me of the same stone that
was on Dad's wedding band. I guess now we all matched.

"As you girls go off on your journeys together, I want you
to always cherish the bonds of sisterhood. With these items,
may you be protected from negative energies wherever
you go." She kissed us both on the forehead, leaving behind
a bright cherry red lipstick smudge, her signature color.

Classic Aunt Rosa, always managing to make the awkward fights between Abuela and Mom a little bit better. I
put the pendant around my neck and felt instantly calmer.
It made me think of the one Suzanne La Luca's aunt had
given her. I wasn't exactly convinced that a matching gem-
stone jewelry set was going to help my relationship with

Magdalena. We were too much of a lost cause, but at this point, it couldn't hurt.

"Very kind of you, Rosa," Dad said.

"Oh! And I have something for you girls from your uncles Raul and Julian who couldn't be here tonight." Uncle Esteban reached for something underneath the kitchen island. It was a glass tank.

"What is it?" I put my face up against the warm glass to get a better look inside. The tank was filled with sand and rocks and some sort of lumpy speckled lizard that was sunbathing beneath the orange glow of a heat lamp.

"A spotted leopard gecko. Your uncles wanted to make sure you had a friend for your new home." Uncle Esteban tapped the glass. "They're supposedly pretty easy to take care of as long as you make sure you feed it live crickets."

I shuddered. I was not a fan of bugs.

"I want him, I want him!" Magdalena squeaked. "I'll name you Chorizo."

He did kind of look like a tiny sausage with legs. I was actually relieved Magdalena called dibs on our new pet because I really didn't have any interest in owning anything that ate crickets.

"I think this is a good note to go to bed on." Dad yawned.

"We all need to get a good night's rest for the big move tomorrow."

"I'll be sure to see you girls off in the morning," Abuela added. "It's time for me to start putting my curlers in! You know how I need my beauty rest."

I didn't understand how she slept in those every night. She always loved to look her best.

"Un besito, Mango," Abuela said to our cockatiel who was now scaling the side of his cage. He made three clicking noises to mimic the sound of kisses. That bird was seriously well trained. Sometimes I wished Magdalena were more like Mango.

Magdalena and I elbowed each other the entire way up to our bedroom. One of the only perks of moving to the new house was that I wasn't going to have to share a room with my sister anymore. Mom had forced us to share for years in an attempt to make us get along, and she probably hoped it would make us "regular kids" or something. I can confidently say that none of those things happened—Magdalena and I aren't friends, I have powers, and she's definitely not normal. What a waste of all those extra bedrooms in Abuela's house.

Now that we were going to actually be living in California suburbia, Mom was letting us have separate rooms. Finally. I hoped this meant Magdalena's prank reign of terror would come to an end, but I doubted it.

As I crawled under the covers, I couldn't believe that tomorrow I would be leaving behind the beautiful beaches of Miami and heading to California, a friendless and empty place where I knew nobody. My life was officially over.

I was seriously going to miss this house and all of the spirits I'd met here in the short amount of time that I'd had my powers.

I waited until Magdalena was asleep before I turned over to my desk drawer to grab my journal. I covered my head with the blankets and began to write about all the things I would miss, which was pretty much everything.

As I signed my name at the bottom of the page, I felt a hot, sticky breath on the back of my neck. I turned to see my annoying sister's pasty white face just inches from my shoulder.

"Whatcha writing?" she said.

"None of your business." I pulled the blankets off us and slammed my journal in my drawer.

5

SPIRIT MIRROR

The next morning I trudged down the stairs, yawning as I went. It felt extra unfair that I had to be awake if the sun wasn't even up yet. As a sign of my protest against going, I decided that I was going to stay in my pajamas for the entire trip. It was too early for regular clothes anyway and I was willing to take the chance of my ghost wandering around in pajamas forever. At least I'd be comfortable. Abuela liked to emphasize the importance of looking our best in the event of spontaneous death. I was pretty sure her worst fear was crossing over and being stuck in an ugly outfit for the rest of her days. I usually tried to keep this in mind when I was getting dressed in the morning, but today was not that day.

Abuelito stood in the kitchen making torrejas, my favorite, and way better than French toast. It was a recipe he picked up from his El Salvadorian neighbor when he first came to this country. The sweet aroma of oil and sugar on the pan made my stomach growl. I watched his pale crinkled hands sprinkle the final dusting of cinnamon on each one. I was going to miss his cooking most of all. Dad was a chef too, but there was something about Abuelito's food that felt like home. Before he met Abuela and began touring the world with her, he used to own a restaurant in Little Havana. He'd always brag about how it was the best Cuban restaurant in town, but that he'd turned in his apron for love so that he could travel with Abuela on all her tours. Such a romantic.

"Now remember what I told you," Abuela placed her cup of café con leche back on the kitchen counter next to Abuelito.

I stared at her closely, trying to fix her in my memory. This wasn't Gloria Jimenez, the famous medium. This was Abuela, wearing her housecoat that smelled of lavender. Her dark gray hair rolled up in curlers from the night before.

I was going to miss her. So much.

"You are destined for great things. Just be sure to follow

the rules and you can never go wrong. And you know I am always one mirror message away." She patted my cheek, catching a few tears that had fallen.

"Let's go, girls, we don't want to miss our flight," Mom said. The dark circles under her eyes that popped against her medium brown skin told me she didn't get much sleep.

I shoved a few torrejas into my mouth and gave my grandparents one last hug before running to the car. It felt like each one of Abuela's statues in the atrium were sending us off as we rushed past them. The sunrise began to cast its early morning rays onto the day and I spent the entire car ride staring out the window at the rows of palm trees we passed by.

We might've left Abuela behind at the house, but her presence came with us. Our driver apparently was a huge Gloria Jimenez fan and wouldn't stop asking questions about growing up around her brilliance. By the time we got to the airport, Mom was in such a sour mood that I knew the rest of the trip was going to be rough.

"This is exactly the reason why we need to get out of this place," she huffed as soon as she got our bags out of the trunk of the car. "We can't keep living in my mom's shadow for the rest of our lives. I'm so tired of people recognizing us. Tired of being the daughter of the world's greatest psychic pain in the neck!"

I personally loved it when people at school asked me what it was like being related to the most famous medium in the entire world, but Mom did not share that joy. She was always a hater about everything.

No one said anything else until we made it past the security check.

"You girls need to use the restroom before we catch our flight?" Dad asked as he put his arm around Mom, trying to calm all her angry muttering. His dark wavy hair was sticking out in all directions.

"Uhhh, I guess." I looked over to the bathroom sign a few feet away.

"Just be sure to take your sister with you," Mom said.

I grabbed Magdalena by the hand and walked with her into the girl's room. Goose bumps covered my arms as soon as we walked through the door.

Turned out it wasn't an air conditioner malfunction causing the near-arctic temperature. It was a spirit! A semi-translucent woman hovered by the sinks without a reflection in the mirror.

As soon as I caught her gaze, I could feel the nervous excitement bubble up in my stomach. This was my chance to do a real-life reading like Abuela! The only thing I needed to figure out was how I should approach her. Not everyone believed in ghosts after all.

The spirit floated beside a sad-looking woman in athletic apparel with a messy bun on top of her head. She washed her hands slowly, staring absently at her own tired reflection. Pink splotches freckled her white skin. I watched her closely, suddenly afraid.

Most of Abuela's clients wanted to speak to a spirit. I had no idea how to casually tell someone they had a spirit standing next to them. She was definitely going to think I was weird. But Abuela would've wanted me to help this woman. This was my WWAD (what would Abuela do) moment. I let go of Magdalena's hand, told her to use the first stall, then walked over to the woman and spirit.

"Excuse me." I tapped the woman on the shoulder.

"The rest of the sinks work just fine," she said, pulling her shoulder away from me.

"Oh, no, that isn't what…" I watched in the mirror as my light brown complexion got paler by the second. I was going to have to just come right out and say it. At least I was pretty sure that's what Abuela would do in this situation. I took a deep breath. "There's someone standing next to you, and I think they want to talk."

"You mean, you?" The woman knit her brow as she turned toward me.

Okay, message not well received. Got it.

"No, not me," I stammered. Abuela always made approaching people look so easy. *C'mon, don't fail at this, Paloma. Make Abuela proud.* "It's a ghost. Well, actually, it's the spirit of someone who was close to you when they were alive. They want to talk to you about something, but they're having a hard time connecting. If you'd like, I could ask them a few questions."

"Is there something wrong with you?" Her eyebrow hitched.

"Umm…no." I gulped.

"You have some wild imagination, kid." She sighed. "But I do have some time to kill before my flight, so I'll bite. What is this ghost trying to say?"

She dried her hands on a paper towel, then turned to face me. She had that "I'm waiting" expression that Mom usually gave me when she wanted me to explain why I got such a bad grade in math.

A small crowd started to gather around us. I felt all of their eyes on me as I stood there trying to think of what to say next. Why wasn't the spirit saying or doing anything?! Then I remembered my new medium tools from Abuela.

"Just one moment please!" I put my backpack on the floor and began to rummage through the spare clothes I shoved in there before we left.

Where were my gifts from Abuela? I frantically buried my arm deeper until I felt the cool metal of the spirit mirror. Perfect!

I held up the compact to my mouth. "Are you having trouble communicating?"

The black obsidian revealed text from the spirit that read, *I am here to talk to my friend Lizzy but she isn't responding to me.*

"I can help you with that." I closed the compact.

The spirit grew slightly more opaque. She was drawing more strength from the energy in the room.

"Okay," the spirit said, nodding. "I'm ready."

I was kind of relieved that I didn't have to keep pausing to read what was on the spirit mirror. I wasn't sure Lizzy would have the patience for that. How did Abuela make it look so easy?!

"Spirit," I annunciated clearly in my grandest Abuela voice possible. "Can you please identify yourself and your relationship to the woman you're standing beside?"

I was pretty sure the whole bathroom was wondering what was going on at this point.

Falling orchid petals swarmed the spirit who stood there in her ripped jeans and cropped-band tee, completely oblivious to the fact that she was standing in the middle of a flower tornado. I could feel myself breaking out in stress hives. This wasn't one of the flowers that I knew by heart.

I plucked *The Book of Flowers* from my bag and desperately flipped through the pages until I finally found what I was looking for—orchids, the symbol of pure friendship.

"Lizzy and I grew up together." The spirit turned to face her friend.

"Looks like it's a close friend of yours," I said. "Someone you've known since childhood. Did you lose your best friend, Lizzy?"

Lizzy looked startled at the sound of her name.

"How did you…" She gazed around the room, then looked back at me. I was pretty sure she believed me now. I could tell I had her full attention at this point. "My best friend, Emily, was supposed to come on this trip with me. We planned it last year, but she died suddenly a few months ago. She never even told me she was sick."

"That would explain why she came to be with you," I said. "She wanted to let you know that she is watching over you and that she's with you on this trip like you both had planned."

Emily smiled and nodded. I'd gotten it right!

"That sounds like her." Lizzy wiped her eyes. "She was always like a protective older sister toward me."

"Please tell her that I am literally with her in spirit," Emily said. "Travel is much cheaper when you're a ghost. Didn't have to waste any sky miles or anything!"

We both chuckled.

The image of orchids swirled into visions of butterfly weed and thyme. Symbols for letting go and courage.

"Emily says that you should be happy that she's now a cheaper travel companion," I said. "But mostly, she wants you to know that she is always with you."

Lizzy wrapped her arms around me and sobbed.

"Thank you, thank you, thank you! I cannot tell you how much I needed to hear that." She held up her hand where

Emily was standing. I nodded as Emily touched hands with her friend.

Pride welled up in my body like air inflating a balloon. The bathroom crowd applauded. I was also pretty sure I heard someone in the crowd compare me to "the great Gloria Jimenez." A total win. My first-ever reading was a success, and I did it without any help!

Everything was going perfectly—until I looked around the room and realized I'd lost Magdalena.

"Shoot," I said. "Got to go!"

I darted out of the bathroom and saw Magdalena had rejoined my parents by the security check. Mom looked madder than usual, her light brown skin now flushed.

That little tattletale. Of course, she snitched on me to Mom.

"Hi, Mom! Hi, Dad! Can't wait to get on that plane, right?" The words poured out of my mouth faster than usual. "We should probably head toward our gate. Don't want to miss our flight!"

If I just acted like nothing was wrong, they'd never know I did a reading. Maybe never acknowledge it.

"Not before we have a bit of a talk, young lady."

My heart sank. She'd used Mom-Voice.

"Oh?" I said, trying to play it cool. "What about?"

"What took you so long in the bathroom, Paloma?" Mom's fingers tapped against her elbow.

If she was expecting a confession, she wasn't getting one. I squirmed under her gaze, hoping it implied I'd had some serious gastro distress. "Sometimes you've just gotta take a long time in a bathroom."

"And it had nothing to do with abandoning your little sister to play medium with strangers?" She was practically shouting now. "Do you know the kind of danger you put yourself in? How many times do I need to tell you to not talk to people that you don't know? So irresponsible!"

Irresponsible? How was helping people irresponsible? How was connecting sad people with their long-lost best friends something to be mad at? If only Mom could under-stand for a fraction of a second how good it felt to make somebody's day better then maybe she'd spend less time being mad at me. And how was Magdalena running away *my* fault? She could have waited for me. She should be the one who was in trouble, not me!

"You're just jealous. I can see ghosts and you can't," I barked. "That's what this is really about isn't it?"

The airport felt as sterile as Mom's feelings toward me in that moment.

She took a deep breath and rubbed her temples, a sign that she was majorly stressed. She was always getting bad migraines when she was really angry.

"I know you like to *think* you can just do everything your Abuela does," she said, "but you need to be more careful. Don't do anything like that again, do you hear me, young lady?"

"Yes, Mom," I barely mumbled. I glanced over at Dad, who was currently spinning his wedding band between his fingers. He shook his head.

Jeez, thanks for the support.

"Your Mom's right on this one," Dad chimed in, slipping his ring back on his finger. "Talking to strangers is no joke, especially for a girl your age."

"I guess." I glared at my sister for tattling.

"I was so scared, Mommy." Magdalena hugged Mom's torso.

"Of course you were, baby," Mom said.

She stuck her tongue out at me while in Mom's embrace. How did my parents never see this? Ugh! It took all of the willpower I had in my body not to scream.

"Excuse me." A woman waved from a distance. "Excuse me!" she shouted louder as she got closer to us. "Is this your daughter?"

She was pointing right at me! It was Lizzy, the woman from the bathroom.

Mom's head jerked up. "Why yes, yes she is. Has she caused you any trouble?"

"Not at all," Lizzy said. "Exactly the opposite. I came over here to tell you what a special young lady you have. You must be very proud."

That's right! You tell them, Lizzy!

"How nice of you to say." Mom's flat tone meant she wasn't interested in continuing this conversation. "Well, I hope you have a lovely flight now." Aka *we aren't talking about this anymore* in Mom-speak.

"You too!" Lizzy beamed as she walked away toward her gate.

I didn't care what Mom said. Lizzy had been so upset earlier, and now she actually smiled for the first time since I met her fifteen minutes ago! That had to be worth something.

"Now boarding for the 9:15 flight to Los Angeles," the disembodied voice called out from over the speaker system.

I huffed my way past the other passengers as well as several ghosts in full-blown tourist attire who had made their way onto the airplane. Once we were finally on board and taking off, the reality of leaving Miami really sank in. I watched the clouds drift by, hoping they would shape themselves into flowers and give me a message that we should turn back.

Come on universe, do your thing! All I needed was one sign that we should have never left Miami.

But nothing happened.

I yanked down the tray in front of me, which was still covered in crumbs from the last flight, and took my new notebook from Abuela out of my backpack.

I wrote at the top of the page:

California…what is my future here?

I'd already been lucky once today with the reading I gave in the bathroom. Why not try a prediction for myself? After all, Abuela said it would help if I practiced controlling my flower premonitions. Within moments, images of flowers danced around the page. I couldn't believe that actually worked! I started to draw and label them according to *The Book of Flowers*. Some of the obvious ones I already knew, like peony, the symbol for a happy life. Definitely not the kind of bleak messaging I had hoped for. This reading wasn't off to a great start.

Zinnia—thoughts of absent friends
Valerian—readiness
Marjoram—joy
Geranium—true friendship

Well, what do I know anyway? I thought to myself as I slammed my book closed. I sighed and stared out the window. Maybe the high altitudes were messing with my psychic powers. I'd have to try again when we landed.

6

Rancho Cucamonga

The taxi pulled up to our new house in the concrete-covered suburban outskirts of the city—Rancho Cucamonga. Where were the estates? Where were the gated communities? Where were the trees? And no beach in sight!

I couldn't believe I was going to be living here. This was much worse than anything I could have ever imagined.

"We finally made it!" Mom smiled.

I didn't know her face could do that. Surely, she wasn't looking at the same house that I was. This place was definitely not smile-worthy.

All the houses on the block pretty much looked the

same. A row of boring beige rectangles with windows. The only difference was that our boring beige rectangle had a slightly more overgrown lawn than the rest. Also the flowers in our window boxes were definitely dead, which really added to the sadness vibes. It looked like an abandoned shack from a postapocalyptic movie.

Okay, maybe I was exaggerating just a little bit.

But still, it wasn't Abuela's place. Although I was pretty sure I still would have disliked it even if it were an exact replica of her house in Miami.

The more I looked at it, the harder it was for me to imagine how Magdalena and I wouldn't be sharing rooms. This place was seriously tiny.

On the bright side, the neighborhood was super haunted, which meant I'd be able to practice talking to ghosts! A pair of eager-looking spirits stared out the window next to the front door. Bet they were looking forward to the new company. I know I was. Abuela always said that communicating with the spirits was like learning any language, it took practice to get good at it. If only I had applied that method to my Spanish classes, maybe I'd have better grades.

A group of teenage ghosts skateboarded down the

street. I waved as they passed by. "At least this town seems spirited!"

"I did not move us all the way across the country for you to make friends with ghosts, Paloma. Save your enthusiasm for making new friends with real living people." Mom scanned the block to make sure the neighbors weren't around to see me waving at an empty street. "You're here so that you and your sister can focus on school and not end up like your cousins. Reality TV stars on that horrible show, *Underbaked*. I don't know how your Aunt Rosa puts up with watching her kids make fools of themselves in the kitchen."

I didn't get what the problem was. My cousins were good cooks. They learned everything from Abuelito. Plus, it wasn't like the show had bad reviews or anything. *Underbaked* was a spin-off of the old popular series, *Fake It til You Bake It*. The judges had to guess which contestant was the professional baker and which one was faking it. Everyone in our family was a total foodie, so being on a show like that was a big deal. And my cousins even made it all the way to the final round! I was pretty sure Mom was just against anything fun. She especially didn't like anything that brought our family added attention, which included reality TV.

"Look, we've all had a long trip," Dad interjected, taking his wedding band off his finger to inspect it before putting it back on again. "Paloma, you sure like to get under your mom's skin, but give it a rest, mija. Please. I'd like for us to start this new chapter off right. Let's go inside like a nice, happy, *normal* family."

He emphasized the word *normal* for Mom's sake. I was sure of it.

"Yeah, Paloma, why do you have to be so weird all the time?" Magdalena teased.

If we were to get into it, I wouldn't be considered the weird one in this family. By far.

As we walked inside, I puffed out my chest and shouted, "Hello, Spirits of Rancho Cucamonga! My family and I are the new residents of this home! Feel free to talk to me anytime! I am always open for conversation."

Okay, maybe I was trying to get under Mom's skin with that one, but to be fair, she started it!

"Paloma, your room is right around the corner. You can go and stay there until dinner," Mom commanded.

I should have expected that.

I marched down the hallway and slammed the door only to discover there weren't any locks! What was the point of having my own room if I couldn't even lock the door! How was I supposed to keep Magdalena out?

It was barely even Day 1 at the new house and I was already confined to the cell of my bedroom until dinner-time. I didn't care what my flower predictions said on the plane, this place was the actual worst.

I decided that if I couldn't be in Miami, the next best thing was to be surrounded by things that reminded me of Miami. And since I had a few hours until dinner, I started to unpack. At least it gave me something productive to do. I looked for the hatbox Abuela had given me and placed it on the shelf in the back of my closet, next to a photograph of the two of us and surrounded it with some candles, unlit of course. I made sure to put it in a special spot so Magdalena wouldn't be able to find it.

I was glad to see that some of my houseplants and succulents had arrived safely. I inspected each one for signs of distress, such as brown leaf tips or drooping, as I arranged them on my windowsill. Thankfully they all looked pretty healthy. My beloved snake plant, Oscar, got a special place on my bedside table. Oscar's planter had been decorated with two large googly eyes to give him extra personality and a tiny Cuban flag poking out of the soil. After making sure each of my plants was sufficiently watered, I hung my fairy lights on the walls to create the perfect mood. The room was starting to feel a little more like home and— dare I say—cottagecore chic. My favorite aesthetic.

Once I had finished unpacking, I plopped on my bed, trying to figure out how all of this was real life right now. It was only a few short months ago that I thought I would be in Miami forever. Right by Abuela's side.

The second I lay on my bed and shut my eyes, I was startled awake by something rapping at my window.

"Magdalena, leave me alone. Stop trying to prank me." My eyes were still fixed on the spider crawling across the ceiling. "I'm not in the mood right now. And I need to get rid of that spider."

"It sounds to me like you've had yourself a bit of a day."

That was *not* my sister.

I sprang up, spotting a middle-aged woman with permed hair, wearing blue hospital scrubs tapping at the glass. I recognized her as one of the spirits I had seen earlier.

"Oh! Hi!" I walked over and opened the window. Half of her body was sticking out of a hydrangea bush.

"You know, you are the first person I've met that can actually see me! I thought it would be nice to pop by and give you a little housewarming hello." The ghost glided to the top of the shrub where she was now sitting. The branches bowed slightly under her weight. "It can be so boring to live in a place where no one knows you exist! Can't tell you how many times I tried opening cabinets and making loud banging noises just to get SOME attention around here. But now, I can finally have a conversation with a real living person! This is the best thing to happen to me in decades!"

Abuela always said that spirits that have stayed in a certain place for an extended period of time were a lot more powerful. That must explain why she was able to tap on my window and bend the branches.

"You're probably the only other person in this house besides me who's excited about this," I said. "My parents and sister don't exactly approve."

"Sorry to hear that," the spirit said as she sniffed one of the hydrangeas. "I can't help but feel that having a new friend to talk to is definitely great news. I'm Beryl by the way, original owner of the house you are now living in." She tugged at the bottom of her hospital scrubs, trying to straighten out a wrinkle that immediately bounced back the second she stopped fiddling with it.

"Nice to meet you," I said.

"You don't sound too happy to be here," Beryl pointed out. "How is the move going?"

"This whole thing has been really hard to wrap my head around, especially the fact that I'm not going to get to see my friends anymore." I poked one of Oscar's googly eyes to make myself feel a little better. It wobbled slightly.

"Well, you have a phone, don't you?" Beryl said. "Why don't you just call them? I hear keeping in touch these days is easier than ever."

"Good point. I did tell my friends I'd call them as soon as I got here," I said.

"I'll leave you to it then!" Beryl slinked back into the shrub and out of sight.

I picked up my phone and video-called Jasmin and Keisha. They both answered right away.

"Hey, guys." I waved my free hand at the camera.

"Hey, Paloma!" They both shouted over each other.

It was nice to see their smiling faces on the screen beaming back at me.

"How's that Hollywood life going?" Keisha asked. "Meet any celebrities yet?"

"Of course she hasn't!" Jasmin said. "She would have told us by now!"

"We have only been on the phone with her for like five seconds, Jasmin." Keisha shook her head.

I could tell she was at the beach by the way the bright Miami sun shined in the background.

"I miss you both so much." I flopped back onto my bed. "And as for the celebrities, the answer is no. The whole point of Mom making us move here was to get away from all that, remember? Apparently, I'm supposed to be living a quiet life where all I do is study and go to church group and not talk to ghosts ever. On the bright side, at least I have my own room."

I scanned my phone camera around the room for them to see. I was glad I took the time to decorate.

"That really stinks. Sorry, dude." Keisha winced. "But your room is looking supercute! Loving the vibes."

"Sounds way worse than being back here for sure," Jasmin added. "Also agreed. Great decor. You settled in fast!"

"It is definitely way worse," I said. "And thanks! I'm already grounded to my room so I figured I may as well unpack."

"Maybe just try giving the place a chance." Keisha was always trying to put a positive spin on things. "Who knows, you may end up liking your new school. I googled Sequoia Academy this morning and to be honest, it looks pretty great. Did you know the place has a greenhouse? Doesn't that sound like your kind of thing?"

"Totally!" Jasmin moved her face closer to the screen. "We know how much this girl loves her plants. Like of course she already has some hanging up in her room. But seriously wow. I wish our school had a greenhouse. Beats outdoor lockers any day. Now you're making me want to go to school there!"

"I know you are just trying to make me feel better, but I appreciate you both trying to cheer me up." I smiled. "Also, for the record, I liked our outdoor lockers."

"Of course!" Keisha said. "That's what we're here for."

"Oh no." Jasmin scrunched her face. "Keisha, we have to go. We have to get stuff together for the party we're throwing for Eloise later."

"You're right! I almost forgot about that," Keisha said,

now power walking down the boardwalk. "Sorry, Paloma. Gotta go. Good luck at school and stuff! Tell us everything. Don't forget the details!"

"Who's El—" The call ended before I could finish my question.

Did they really replace me with a new friend that quickly? I'd only been gone half a day!

Guess their lives were moving on without me. A pit burned in my stomach. This whole thing stunk.

7

The Greenhouse

The next morning felt like the first day of the end of my life. At least I picked out the perfect first day of school outfit: a high-waisted pair of vertically striped rainbow shorts, high-tops and a bright yellow shirt with a giant daisy on the front that went perfectly with my amethyst necklace from Aunt Rosa. I may not have been excited about going to my new school, but at least I was going to be fashionable. Representing Miami always!

At the bus stop, I noticed all of the other kids had the same kind of madras shorts, polo shirts, and boat shoes as everyone else.

I shuddered. These were—dare I say it—preppies. I'd always thought the preppy look was more of an East Coast thing, but apparently the kids at this school didn't get that memo.

I made a point of sitting in the back. I wasn't in the mood to be friendly just yet anyway. I also wasn't confident that I would know how to talk to anyone even if I wanted to. Back in Miami, making friends was easy because I never really had to try. Everyone already knew who I was because of Abuela, so I always had classmates coming up to me to ask about her. But here, I was just some awkward new girl sitting alone at the back of the bus.

After about fifteen minutes, we pulled up to a large brick building surrounded by the most beautiful landscape architecture I had ever seen. And trust me, I knew plants. The outer turrets of the facade were flanked by tall cypresses and a rose garden walkway lined the pathway from the bus drop-off station to the front door. There was even a labyrinth made from rows of well-groomed boxwoods that spelled out the schools initials *SA* for Sequoia Academy. This place clearly took their plants seriously.

The inside was somehow even nicer. I half expected sad linoleum floors and dirty lockers typical of the public schools back home, but instead I saw carved wooden stairwells and marble columns. I guess Keisha was right. This place was fancy. No outdoor lockers though. Points lost there.

I looked at my phone and realized I had some time to kill before my first class, so I decided to do a little exploring. I figured the greenhouse had to be around here somewhere. That would be the true test of this place's devotion to botanicals. It was one thing to have a nice garden, but greenhouses were a whole other situation. The temperatures had the potential to get superhot, so it was important to make sure the flowers stayed nice and hydrated, or else everything would just end up looking like wilted crisps. Mom had a mini one back at her shop in Miami where we kept all the tropical plants that liked things extra hot.

I walked down the long hallways, getting distracted by the buzz of students trading the latest gossip and "who did what" over the summer. It reminded me of Jasmin and Keisha and all the things we'd discuss on the first day back to school. It felt strange not knowing anybody's name. Part of me wondered: Do I even know how to make friends on my own, without Abuela's celebrity?

After what felt like a thousand hours of looking for the

greenhouse, I was almost ready to give up when I finally stumbled across a large room, the size of a cafeteria. The ceiling was covered in sheets of glass that looked out to the sky. I was in total awe. Large flower baskets suspended from beams surrounded me. The English ivy and purple heart plants cascaded downward like tiny waterfalls. Some of them had clearly been there for a while and had managed to twist their way around the light fixtures. I noted overgrowth at the back of the room that could do with a little pruning, but other than that, this place was perfect.

As I walked deeper into the greenhouse, I noticed a boy around my age sitting at one of the long wooden tables. He wore the same kind of preppy attire as the other students, a burgundy-and-navy-striped rugby shirt with a white collar and khakis. There was a familiar translucent nature to his appearance.

A surge of joy rushed through me like a caffeine energy boost. This was the most ghost encounters I'd had in such a short amount of time! Abuela was right about California being a hot spot for spirit activity.

"Hi, it's so nice to meet you! I'm Paloma." I extended my hand to shake his before remembering it would pass right through. I quickly jammed it into my pocket instead. "Got any tips for a newbie? I just started here today!"

"You can see me?" He blinked heavily.

Right, I forgot that not all ghosts were used to talking to living people.

"Yeah, it's kind of my thing now," I explained. "Sorry if I startled you. I've been testing out the new powers ever since they kicked in over the summer. I'm still pretty new to the whole talking to ghosts thing."

"Wow, that's awesome!" he said. "I guess you could say I'm pretty new at the whole talking to alive people thing, so we can figure it out together! My name's Dustin. Used to be a student at this place. You said today is your first day here?"

"It is!" I said. "I'm from Miami originally."

"Super rad. Well I am glad you're here now. It'll be nice to have someone to actually talk to." He floated over to a sculpted Japanese cedar that was manicured to look like some sort of a fish. "So, what made you decide to check out the greenhouse anyway? Most students never come in here outside of class time."

"I just thought I'd check it out. I used to work with my mom at her flower shop, so you can say I'm kind of a plant enthusiast." I walked over to smell the chrysanthemums. "This place is beautiful. I can't believe they have classes in here."

"Yeah, it's my favorite room in the school, which is why I spend most of my time in here. There's even an agricultural lab where you actually get to grow plants from cuttings to take home with you," Dustin said. "And they have a class on food production where you can learn about the whole farm-to-table process. Oh, and then there's the drought resistant plant club, of course. It's pretty interesting stuff if you're into that sort of thing."

"That does sound cool!" I was definitely into that sort of thing. I turned my body so he could see my backpack, which was completely covered in botanical pins. "I'll have to see if I can get that put on my schedule!"

"You should." Dustin hovered near one of the many hanging baskets in the room. "Though the class does fill up pretty quick."

"Hmmm…that's surprising." I watched him inspect the purple heart plant. I was pretty sure I was the only plant geek back at my school in Miami.

"Environmental stuff is super big here." Dustin floated

back down to the ground level, hovering just above a bed of cacti. He eyed me seriously.

I hated to admit to myself that this place was starting to win me over.

Ring!!!

"Oh no! Please tell me that wasn't the bell for homeroom," I said. "Do you know where room 107 is?"

I had been so busy looking for the greenhouse that I didn't check to see where any of my classes were.

"Down the hall and to the right," he said, gesturing in the direction of my classroom. "Can't miss it, though you might want to power walk. The teachers are pretty strict about lateness around here."

"Thanks for the tip!" I yelled as I sprinted toward my first class.

Late on the first day! I reprimanded myself. *Mom is going to kill me if she finds out about this.*

After homeroom, I decided to do a little more exploring. The halls were filled with the school's resident ghosts and I couldn't wait to talk to them all. Like Barry Sanchez, the hall monitor who spent decades of his life keeping order in the halls of Sequoia Academy and still took his job very seriously, even after death.

"Eres una bruja?" He looked surprised when I reacted to him yelling at me for running to my next class.

"I'm not a witch, I can just talk to ghosts!" I smiled.

"Sorry, you're the first person to listen to me in half a century." Barry chuckled.

It felt like I was fitting in more with the ghosts than the other students. Without my connection to Abuela, I was as invisible to the other students as Barry, who was still determined to tell kids who couldn't even hear him to slow down.

There was still so much of this place I wanted to check out. And since I still had some time before my next class, I decided to see what other ghosts were lurking around.

In the auditorium, I ran into the ghost of Miss Lucy Lammermoor, a tall, slender spirit wrapped in a bright orange shawl that popped against her black jumpsuit. Her salt-and-pepper hair was pinned up in a thick bun on top of her head. According to Barry, Lucy Lammermoor was the former theatre arts teacher who liked to spend her afterlife adding a little dose of mayhem to all the theatre productions.

"An actress must be prepared for anything!" I heard her say as she knocked over set parts while some of the students rehearsed. I had a feeling she probably would have gotten along with Suzanne La Luca's aunt.

Luckily for me, it appeared that the school was sufficiently haunted, so I was bound to get loads of practice talking to spirits. I'd be ready to go on tour with Abuela in no time!

But as I walked into language arts with Miss Gustavo, it wasn't the ghosts that stood out to me. There was a boy at the back of the room with dark hair, dark jeans, and a vacant expression as he looked out the window. I felt like I had been making the same gloomy face all summer after I found out about the move. All of a sudden, swirls of flowers I didn't recognize circled around him.

As I made my way to my desk, I tried not to stare too much, but it was hard not to. I pulled out my copy of *The Book of Flowers* and started to skim through different pictures to see if I could find out what these meant.

Got it!

Oleander. The symbol for caution. What was that supposed to mean?

SMACK!!!

It turned out that walking and reading at the same time wasn't the greatest idea. I was so lost in a daze that I crashed directly into my desk and face-planted on the floor. *Way to go, Paloma.* And of course, the whole class saw everything.

My cheeks flamed red hot with embarrassment.

Thankfully, a light freckled arm reached down to help me. I looked up to find a friendly face staring back at me. Her curly hair reminded me of mine, only hers was coated with gel which gave them an added crunch.

"Everyone saw that, right?" I sighed as I awkwardly climbed into my desk chair.

"Oh, one hundred percent. But don't stress it too much, this doesn't even land in the top twenty most embarrassing moments that have happened at this school," she reassured me. "I'm Willow Goldstein, by the way. You're new, right?"

"Yeah. Moved here yesterday from Miami. My name's Paloma Ferrer," I said in a low whisper. "Sorry for being such a klutz. Thanks for helping me out."

"We've all been there. My first day here, I fell in the mud during third grade recess. Took almost a year before everyone stopped calling me Mud Stain. I secretly hold a little grudge against the person who started the nickname." She gestured to the boy at the back of the room, who still had flowers popping out of his head. "That's Stephen Sato. He's not exactly the nicest guy in school."

"Yikes," I said. "The mud stain thing makes falling flat on my face sound a little less embarrassing. Although that nickname is some pretty uncreative bullying. It barely even rhymes with your name. I'm not even sure anyone here knows my name to come up with a nickname like that, but maybe it would be something like Paloma Faller instead of Ferrer since I fell. Not that I want a nickname for doing something awkward. Anyway, what I'm trying to say is, I appreciate you for sharing it." Was I talking too much? Definitely. Probably.

Wow, I was really bad at talking to people. Willow was nice enough not to mention it and started telling me more about the school until Miss Gustavo started the lesson.

If I was going to be stuck here, I might as well make some alive friends and not just talk to ghosts all the time. Although part of me didn't want to give Mom the satisfaction of being right!

Halfway through class, exhaustion hit and it took all my will power not to fall asleep at my desk. I couldn't tell if this was medium fatigue or jet lag. Abuela said being around ghosts can be a little draining sometimes, mostly because they actually sucked the energy out of a room, but also because they liked to talk a lot. And I did spend a lot of time talking to Barry and Dustin this morning.

I glanced over my shoulder, stealing another look at Stephen Sato, who was still at the back of the classroom looking out the window. He didn't *look* mean. But then again, Abuela always said looks could be deceiving.

8

A Way Out

"Paloma, I'm very disappointed in your behavior at school today," Mom said as she passed the bowl of arroz con pollo across the table. I made sure my spoonful had an extra helping of peas in the hopes that doing double duty on the vegetables would dilute whatever punishment Mom was about to throw my way.

Her tone didn't come as a surprise. I already knew that my chronic lateness to class was going to get back to her thanks to Dustin's warning that the school was pretty serious about that stuff, even on the first day. I could never catch a break.

"I was hoping for better from you." Mom put her head

in her hands. "Look, I know this move has been hard. It's been hard on all of us. But it would do you some good to at least try to fit in and be on time to your classes."

I should have figured my vegetable trick wouldn't work. Guess peas weren't enough to offset Mom's anger.

"It's easy to get lost in there!" I said defensively. "You can't expect me to know where everything is on day one! And that welcome packet they sent didn't have a map in it."

Which was true, but I left out the part about me being extra chatty with the school ghosts between classes.

"Sequoia Academy's a big place. You need to get used to where everything is. Maybe make a buddy who can show you around," Dad said as he sliced into his piece of chicken. "That helped me when I went to a new school."

Exactly! At least I could always count on Dad to come to my defense. Well, most of the time anyway. I wasn't going to forget the airport incident that easily.

"I made lots of friends today, Daddy!" Magdalena bragged.

"That so?" Dad said. "Well, we are very proud of you, sweet pea. And speaking of peas, Paloma, could you pass some to your sister? I see her rice is lacking some greens."

95

Magdalena's face turned the color of a cranberry as she held back a laugh. I didn't get it. Peas weren't that funny.

I forgot I was still holding the bowl so I scooped a large amount onto my sister's plate, making sure to give her as many peas as possible before I set the bowl back down on the table. She could eat each and every one. Maybe one for each of those new friends she kept bragging about.

"First days are always tough. I think we can cut you some slack just this once, Paloma." He winked. "And honey," he turned to Mom who was still giving me a stink eye, "why don't you tell the girls about your exciting new business venture?"

Her mood immediately shifted. She practically glowed.

"Oh, well it's still early on, but I guess it's worth a little celebrating." Mom pulled out a pair of car keys from her purse. "We are taking Flor's Flowers on the road, kids!" She hugged her keys to her chest.

"Your mom went out and bought a vintage Volkswagen pickup truck that she's going to convert into a flower store on wheels. It's getting delivered tomorrow!" He leaned over and kissed Mom on the cheek. "Isn't that exciting news, girls?"

"That *is* exciting!" I shouted. "Mom, that's seriously so cool."

And I wasn't just trying to get back on her good side. I was actually happy to hear she was back in business. Mom was really good at her job as a florist and personally, being around more flowers would be good for my psychic development. Plus, it would be nice for her to have something else to worry about besides my grades.

"Glad you think so," Mom replied. "Because I could use an extra hand to get it set up."

"Count me in!" I said. "Your flower assistant reporting for duty."

I couldn't believe she was letting me help after the proposal fiasco this summer. As long as I didn't have to trim the roses in flower shop purgatory again, I was all in.

"Flower truck aside, the most exciting part of my day was being able to go grocery shopping without getting stopped by someone who recognized me as the daughter of Gloria Jimenez, medium to the stars!" Mom closed her eyes as if she were relaxing on South Beach bathing in the sun. "I can get used to this. Although I was a little disappointed I couldn't find my Café Bustelo."

"And my exciting news of the day..." Dad did a short

drumroll on the table with his fork and knife before saying, "I'm starting that new job tomorrow as head chef at one of LA's premier restaurants. So as of tomorrow, you girls will be seeing a lot less of me around here."

"Wait, what job?" I blinked rapidly, looking between my parents in confusion.

"You know how I've been spending a lot of time training under your grandpa? That I've been cooking at his friend's restaurant in Miami for the past year?" He raised his eyebrows like we were supposed to know what he was talking about. "Turns out word of my cooking got around. A restaurateur who was planning to open a new location in LA approached me and asked me to come aboard. It's why we moved out here. Could've sworn I must have mentioned it."

He definitely did not mention it.

This was not good. Less Dad meant more Mom and Magdalena, which meant more misery for me.

The news came like a punch to the chest. Because this meant that *Dad* was the reason we left Miami. It couldn't be true. Dad never would have ruined my life like this. Mom must've been behind it somehow. She was the one who was always complaining about living with Abuela. Not Dad. None of this made any sense.

The thought of Dad's betrayal made me nauseated.

"I'm not feeling so great," I said. "If you guys don't mind, I'm going to my room."

"Probably the jet lag, amorita!" Dad said. He stretched his arms. "Haven't recovered myself either, even with that nap I took! Might hit the hay early too."

"Not so fast, young lady," Mom said. "I don't want you to think you're getting off the hook this easily for what happened today."

"Huh?" I asked. "I thought Dad gave me a free pass for the whole being late to class thing."

"I'm not talking about school." Her deep brown eyes felt like they were piercing into my soul.

"Then what?" I was seriously drawing a blank.

"Don't act like you don't know about the live crickets I found in my luggage this morning." She practically spat the words out. "Magdalena already told me that she saw you do it."

I glanced over at Magdalena, who flashed me the wickedest of smiles. Was this why she had been silently laughing all through dinner?

99

"ARE YOU KIDDING ME?" I slammed my hands on the table, making the bowl of arroz con pollo jump in the air. "How is it that you always believe HER? I didn't put disgusting crickets in your luggage. It was obviously Magdalena who did it! She was the one who was excited about feeding crickets to our new pet lizard, not me!"

Both of my parents turned to my sister who did her best impression of an innocent child. One who clearly hated bugs and would NEVER think about picking one up and putting it in her mom's luggage.

Despicable.

"I can't believe you would accuse your sweet little sister like that," Mom said, her voice dripping with disappointment. "You need to learn how to take responsibility for your actions."

"I didn't do it! This is UNREAL!" I shouted. "You always take her side over mine. That's it, I'm going to bed. For real this time."

I huffed down the hallway and into my bedroom, making sure to lean a chair against the doorknob because of the whole no locks situation. I was practically seeing red as I paced around the room in fury. All I wanted was to talk to Abuela or my friends back home, but with the time difference, it was too late for phone calls.

I would give anything to be back in Miami, where I belonged, with Abuela and Uncle Esteban and Aunt Rosa and Maria. I wanted things to be back to the way they were. To hang out on the beach or go to the mall with Jasmin and Keisha. I wasn't even sure where the closest beach was or if we'd even get to go with Mom and Dad so busy now.

I flopped face-first onto my bed and winced as something dug into my leg. It was my spirit mirror in my pocket. I couldn't call Abuela now, but maybe I could send her a spirit mirror message for her to read later!

I pulled out the golden compact and began dictating. Abuela needed to hear about this even if she wouldn't see this until the morning.

Hi Abuela! Sorry, I know it's late. I was wondering if maybe you'd reconsider taking me on your Latin American tour. I need to get out of this place. Pronto. Things in California are worse than you could imagine. Did you know Dad had a job lined up already to come here? What is that about?

Anyway, I really miss you. Send my love to everyone.

This is Paloma by the way. I still don't think I know how this works.

After sending the message, I grabbed my journal and tried to do another self-prediction.

I jotted at the top of the page:

Will I make any friends here?

After a moment of concentrating, the flowers began to appear.

Delphinium—growth and progress
Alstroemeria—friendship, good fortune, and prosperity
Buttercups—childishness

"Childishness?!" That had to be a mistake. My powers probably needed to adjust to the new time zone.

I slammed the notebook in my drawer and stomped over to my closet. This was a complete waste of time.

I needed to do something to clear my head and I knew exactly what would help. I grabbed my pruning shears and made my way outside. There was nothing that made me feel better than a little night gardening.

"I sense some trouble," I heard a man's voice say as I angrily hacked away at an overgrown hedge. It sounded like it was coming from the flower box. A fedora and a set of eyes peeked out from the gardenias that Mom had just planted this morning. It was the only thing in the garden that wasn't struggling to live.

"Can I help you?" My eye twitched as I tried to figure out if this was the same ghost I had seen with Beryl when I first arrived at the house. As much as I enjoyed talking to ghosts, all I wanted was to rage garden in peace.

"The name's Harrison. I'm here for a little neighborly visit from next door," he said. "I'm the uncle of the current occupants. They're new in town too, so I thought I'd keep them company at the new place."

"Well, that was nice of you to swing by," I said.

His thin mustache barely grazed the upper part of his lip. Based on his clothes—an oversized three-piece sharkskin suit and fedora—and well-oiled hair, I'd guess he was from the 1950s. I'd watched enough old movies with Abuela to place that kind of wardrobe.

Even his voice sounded vintage, like he was an old-timey radio broadcaster or something.

"Couldn't resist after I heard all of that commotion," he said. "I've been known in my time to enjoy some neighborhood gossip. So shoot, what's grinding your gears, button?"

I scrunched my nose at the word *button*. Yeah, he for sure wasn't from *this* era. Plus, I didn't love the fact that he had been eavesdropping on our family dinner.

"Family trouble, friend trouble, trying-to-fit-in trouble," Beryl said as she manifested through the neighboring hydrangea bush and took a seat on top. "She's been like this ever since she's gotten here."

So much for alone time.

"Hey!" I shouted.

"It's okay. Being new is tough." She nudged Harrison's arm. "As you should know, being the new ghost on the block."

"She's got a point," Harrison said. "Listen, kid. My advice to you is you gotta try to make the best of whatever situation you're in and get outta your funk. Things will get better eventually. You've just gotta give it some time."

"Who says I'm in a funk?" I pouted.

"I haven't known you for more than two days, and I could tell you that you've been down in the dumps since you got here. I'm not just diagnosing you because I used to be a nurse," Beryl said. "Because that isn't my area of expertise."

"Alright, maybe you're right," I rubbed my glasses on

my shirt before returning them to my face. "But how do I fix it when I don't even want to be here?"

"Try getting involved with something that matters to you to get your mind off things." Beryl floated next to Harrison. "Any after-school activities or organizations that you can join?"

"I guess there are a few options besides the dreaded church choir that Mom has been wanting me to go to," I said. "There's a drought resistance club that sounds cool."

A ping alert sounded from my spirit mirror. A response from Abuela. Wow, she was up late!

It read:

My Darling Paloma, I wouldn't expect you to be settled in after only one day.

Being in a location with a lot of spirit activity means the energy levels are the perfect condition to perform a reading. Be sure to let me know once you've tried one!

An idea hit me like a jolt of lightning.

I hustled back inside, shouting over my shoulder, "Thank you! Good night!" to Beryl and Harrison, who both shrugged and floated away. Once I made it to my room, I grabbed my notebook and started scribbling on the page.

Sure, Abuela completely ignored my request to join

her on tour, but she gave me something even better: an idea for me to help students, one ghost at a time. A way for me to be just like her. Because Abuela was all about helping people.

And if I could do that, then I'd prove to her that I'm ready for more. The tour wasn't until December, so I still had plenty of time. All I had to do was make it happen.

And I had the perfect name for what I was going to do. *TOTALLY PSYCHIC, a social media page for ghost content.* Abuela was going to love this.

Latin American tour here I come.

9

Totally Psychic

I groaned awake to my *new* alarm clock of Beryl shaking my mattress and Harrison slamming the shutters against the windows. This was way worse than sharing a room with Magdalena, which I never thought was possible. All of the blood in my body felt like it had been replaced with a thick molasses. I was so exhausted from staying up all night working on my plan that I could barely motivate myself to open my eyes.

"Guys, what are you doing?" My lashes were practically sealed shut with eye crud. I snatched my glasses from the bedside table and the world shifted into focus.

"Old habits." Beryl shrugged. "When you're used to

being invisible all of the time, you'll resort to just about anything to get a little attention."

"What time did you go to bed last night?" Harrison asked. It was hard to hear him on the other side of the glass.

"I don't know," I yawned. "Maybe close to 4:00 a.m." I had been up all night coming up with plans for Totally Psychic. I had even watched some videos of Abuela's old television program, *Miami Mystic*, in the hopes of gleaning some wisdom. The episodes all look like they were from the '80s or something and were uploaded to YouTube with the supergrainy quality that comes from filming your TV screen with a cell phone. I especially liked how all of the comments were about how Abuela's healing messages helped people through some tough times.

"That's way too late for a girl your age to be going to sleep," Beryl said. "What could you possibly have been up to at that hour?"

"If you must know," I started to comb the unreasonable knots out of my thick, matted hair, which just made it puffier and frizzier. I reached for my water spritzer to rejuvenate the curls. "I came up with a plan to use my gift to help others connect with their loved ones. I'm going to do live readings for my classmates on Instagram!"

The ghosts nodded and congratulated me. Though I could tell by their blank expressions that they didn't have any idea what I was talking about. Before they got a chance to ask me more questions, I grabbed the pile of flyers that I'd been working on all night and raced for the bus.

As soon as I got to school, I hung up my flyers all over the building. I'd drawn pictures all over them of flowers, tarot cards, candles, and anything else I could think of that screamed "psychic." This was exactly the kind of thing that I needed to be doing to get Abuela's attention. If she couldn't see me do readings in real life, she could watch me do them on social media!

Once Barry the hall monitor got wind of what I was doing, he was right on my heels.

"Do you have a permit from the administrative office to hang those?" He tapped his clipboard, attempting to get some extra height by standing on his toes.

I pretended I couldn't hear him as I continued to paste more flyers onto lockers. I did feel a little guilty about what I was doing, but this was important! Barry wouldn't understand. I was going to be giving the first-ever virtual reading in the history of mediums. I didn't have time to get a permit.

"Don't pretend you can't see me, young lady." Barry waved his hands in my face trying to get my attention, I nearly stumbled into one of the other students.

Guess my poker face wasn't as good as I thought. He knew I was ignoring him.

"Okay, fine," I confessed. "I see you, Barry. I don't have a permit, but I promise I'm almost finished putting these up."

"Channeling ghosts are you, bruja?" He raised his eyebrows as he inspected one of the flyers.

"Again…not a witch! And that's the plan," I said.

"Alright, I'll let this go as a warning, but only because you are new here." Barry's eyes darted from the wall back to the large stack of posters that I still had in my hand. We both knew I wasn't close to being finished. "Next time, get a permit. We can't let you get into the habit of breaking the rules, now can we?"

I was glad he decided to take it easy on me, although I wasn't sure how he expected to notify the administration office of what I was up to, given his ghostly condition.

I spent the rest of the morning before homeroom putting up more flyers. I had to get the word out about my psychic skills, and I was surprised that the handle @Totally-Psychic wasn't already taken.

Excitement quickly turned to exhaustion, and by the time I got to second period, I was starting to fall asleep at my desk. The hum of the fluorescent lights definitely wasn't helping things. It droned on like a white noise machine, my eyes getting heavier by the minute.

The rest of my classes melted together in a blur. Anytime I felt like I was dozing off, I jumped up to check on my follower count. It was pretty much the only thing keeping me awake at this point. Thirty-seven already, and it was still early!

Now the only thing I had left to figure out was a location where I could host my first reading. My house was out of the question for obvious reasons since Mom would never approve. So that really only left the school, seeing as how those were the only two locations I actually had access to in the entire state of California.

All I needed now was to find a room with the right acoustics and lighting. It would also need to be unoccupied for most of the day.

The auditorium, while having many positive characteristics, was too noisy with the ghost of Lucy Lammermoor constantly breaking things. I could argue that her disruptions would make for interesting content, but they might dissuade other ghosts from coming through and I couldn't take that risk.

The hallways were off limits because Barry was on constant patrol, and most of the classrooms would be occupied during the day, which really only left one spot.

The greenhouse.

It had the lighting that I was looking for, lots of plants for visual interest, and it was quiet. The only problem was...all that glass. We'd be so exposed. And I bet the school wouldn't be a fan of me channeling ghosts on school property. I also wondered what the cool air from the ghosts coming through would do to the plants.

But it was my best option, so I had to go for it. Abuela would want me to take the risk, wouldn't she?

I decided to do my readings during my lunch period so I wouldn't be missing any classes, but also so I could avoid the embarrassment of sitting alone. Being the new kid at school was extra hard during lunch.

But I still had to eat today. Laughter filled the air as I

walked into the cafeteria. I scanned the room looking for an empty table to sit at when I heard a familiar voice calling from behind me.

"Hey, Paloma!" I nearly dropped my lunch tray at the sound of my name. It was Willow! "Come and sit with me and my friends."

Her smile brought my heart rate back to a normal level. She was waving me over!

"I'd love to." I breathed a sigh of relief. "Thanks, Willow!"

Willow set her tray down and introduced me to Fatima and Thalia. I appreciated their use of bold vibrant colors in their wardrobe and the fact that they were the few people in school not wearing collared shirts! Their outfits were supercute.

I waved hello, which felt a lot more awkward than I intended.

"So, Willow tells me you're sort of famous or something." Fatima tossed one of her long French braided pigtails to the back of her neon yellow windbreaker. "Is that true?"

"Oh, well, yeah kind of. But not me." I twisted my mouth. "It's my grandma who's famous."

Was that why they invited me to come sit with them? I started nervously picking at the black rubber seam on the cafeteria table exposing the layers of laminate wood and particle board.

"We know." Thalia leaned back in her chair. The rear metal legs supported her as she balanced. "We already googled you. Sorry if that's weird, we couldn't resist. It's supercool you have a famous grandpa."

"Grandma," Fatima corrected. She pulled at the split ends of her dark brown hair.

"That's okay," I said. "A lot of people have heard of my abuela."

I put my hands in my pockets in an attempt to look more casual. It also helped me to stop fidgeting, but it did nothing for the sinking feeling in my stomach. Did it matter that they might only be talking to me because of Abuela? At least I wasn't sitting alone…

"Did you hear about the new medium service?" Willow asked. "We figured you might be the one behind it!"

"You caught me." I flashed a cheesy smile. "I'm going to do a live stream of my psychic services tomorrow if I can get anyone interested in signing up."

It was nice to know my flyers were getting some attention!

Fatima stood on her chair. Her brown ankles poked out from a pair of socks that looked like alligator mouths trying to eat her.

"Did you guys hear?" Fatima shouted to the rest of the cafeteria. "Our new friend Paloma is Totally Psychic! She's going to do her first reading tomorrow afternoon. You won't want to miss it."

The rest of the students whooped and cheered. I couldn't tell if it was genuine, but my heart soared regardless. It felt nice to be seen.

The attention was short-lived and soon the rest of the cafeteria went back to their regularly scheduled programming of eating lunch and talking about who had the best summer vacation. That was until Stephen Sato, the boy from my language arts class with a permanent brooding expression on his face and flowers still popping out of his head, strode over to our table.

"What if I told you I don't believe in ghosts?" he shouted, loud enough for the surrounding tables in the cafeteria to hear. A roar of "ooos" followed his comment. It was really hard to take him seriously when he had yellow hyacinths and tansies popping out of his head. I stifled a laugh. I couldn't help it if he looked ridiculous!

He looked me dead in the eye, clearly unamused by the fact that I wasn't intimidated by him. But why should I care if he believed in ghosts or not?

Willow's warning about his bad vibes echoed in my head. I thought back to what I had read in *The Book of Flowers*. Yellow hyacinths symbolized jealousy. And tansies…well, that flower came with more than one meaning. Sometimes there were multiple ways to interpret a flower and this just happened to be one of those flowers. Either he was sending me wishes of good health, which would be super nice of him. Or it was the flower's other meaning: a declaration of war. My gut was telling me it was the second one.

Not good.

"I think you're totally fake and this whole psychic thing is just some made up way for you to get attention," he continued to bellow for everyone to hear. "And *friends* since you have none."

What was this guy's problem?

"Not cool, Stephen," Willow said. "Paloma IS psychic. At least we know her grandma is from what we checked out on the internet. And if the internet says so, I'm sure her powers are legit!"

"If you're so sure I'm a fake then let me do a reading for you," I challenged.

If he wanted to test me then all I needed to do was prove him wrong. Skeptics didn't scare me. Or Abuela.

"Alright, new girl," he said, crossing his arms. "You're on. But if you're a fake, I'm telling the whole school about it."

"You won't have to." I handed him one of my flyers. "Follow my page and meet me in the greenhouse tomorrow at lunch." I wasn't going to let him intimidate me. No matter how rude he might have been. "Don't want you to miss out on getting your mind blown."

"Exactly what she said!" Willow stood up from the table and looked down at Stephen. He was a few inches shorter than she was, but Willow was standing on her tippy-toes to make herself appear even bigger. Kind of like what you would do to prevent a bear attack. (I was pretty sure I read that somewhere when I searched for California survival tips.)

"Plus she's going to have us there to help!" Fatima added.

I was?

"You need a production crew, don't you?" Thalia lifted

her eyebrows. "Lucky for you, we are members of our school's film club."

"We're basically experts with this kind of thing," Fatima confirmed.

I was beginning to feel more confident already.

I may not have been afraid of him, but I didn't imagine I would be doing my first official reading on a dare. If this went terribly, my career as a medium would be over before it even started.

I'd show him. I was totally psychic, and I'd prove this know-it-all bully wrong.

10

The First Reading

It was almost noon the next day and I was already set up to do Stephen Sato's reading in the greenhouse. I made sure to get there early so that everything would be ready. The sun felt hotter than usual as it beat its rays through the glass overhead. A bead of sweat trickled down the side of my face. I used one of Abuela's old tablecloths to drape over one of the picnic tables. And thanks to Willow, Fatima, and Thalia's film club connections, I even managed to get a tripod for my phone to help with recording the reading.

I walked around admiring everything, pretty impressed with the setup. Thalia helped to arrange the hanging plants so that they would act as a backdrop, which was a nice touch. The only thing I still needed to do was light the candles to make sure no bad ghosts would be coming through. Thalia was still making the final touches to her flower arrangement and Fatima was walking around testing the acoustics on the boom microphone. I couldn't believe my first-ever reading was actually happening!

Excitement welled up inside me until Stephen showed up. All that joy immediately crumpled into a giant knot gathered in the pit of my stomach. I anxiously twisted my necklace around my fingers.

"You got this," Willow said from behind the tripod as if she could sense my anxiety. At least I had my new friends here to support me.

Even Dustin gave me a reassuring thumbs-up as he hovered near a yucca tree that looked like it could use a little bit of watering.

"Look," I said, taking a deep breath as soon as Stephen was close enough to hear me. "I know you made it super clear yesterday that you don't believe in this stuff, but I need you to try to be just a little open to it for the sake of the reading."

Doing a reading for skeptics was always extra hard because ghosts didn't like to waste their energy crossing over for people who didn't even believe they existed. No one likes a one-sided relationship, even ghosts.

"Yeah, yeah, yeah. Whatever." Stephen looked up at the ceiling. "Just get this over with so I can move on with my day. The rest of the school's going to see right through this act and know that this is bogus."

If he was trying to look disinterested in being here, he was succeeding.

"Let's do this." I glared in his direction, then gave Willow the nod to click the Go Live button.

We were officially streaming.

"Hello to the students of Sequoia Academy! New student Paloma Ferrer here to share with you a spirit reading for one of our classmates," I announced. "Our guest today is Stephen Sato who was very generous to volunteer for this. Let's see who comes through for him shall we?"

I closed my eyes and concentrated, the way Abuela always did when she hosted her readings. Within a few moments, the room went icy cold and I clearly wasn't the only one in the room that could feel it since everyone suddenly started rubbing their arms for warmth. My entire body was peppered with goose bumps, which made me quickly realize that I forgot to wear a sweater. Rookie mistake. I made a mental note to bring one next time. But more importantly, the chill meant that the portal had been opened and our ghost would be arriving any second. I couldn't believe it! This was really going to work!

The spirit that came through was an older woman with a medium-length pin-straight black bob hairdo and a Pepto-Bismol–pink dress that remained stiff despite her movements as she floated over to where Stephen was sitting. Her outfit looked like it was made out of a thick curtain-like material with a giant bow stitched in the center.

"Is that my little squish butt sitting there?" the spirit said adoringly. She adjusted the pillbox hat to stop it from sliding off her head, but every time she let go, it migrated right back to where it had been in the first place.

I suppressed a laugh. What did she just call him?

"What's so funny?" Thalia whispered to me.

I could see Fatima giving her a dirty look as she pointed at the microphone. She must have picked that up on the boom.

"For the viewers who are wondering what is going on, we have a spirit that came through for Stephen who seems to be very close to him. I just need to ask her again what

she said to make sure I am sharing the right information."
I remembered that they were only able to hear my half of
the conversation!

"I'm sorry, can you repeat that?" I directed my question toward the spirit. I was positive I must not have heard her right.
My viewership numbers were increasing by the second.

"My nephew, Stephen," the spirit said, a little louder
this time. Her tone was much more serious than it had
been before. "He had the cutest little squishy butt when
he was born, and I've called him that ever since. I have
special auntie privileges to do so."

She said it so matter-of-factly that I guess she didn't see
anything funny about that nickname.

"What is it?" Stephen squirmed in his chair. "Why are
you laughing?"

"I don't want to say." Part of me wanted to spare him
the embarrassment. The other part of me couldn't stop
laughing.

"Why? Because you know you're a fraud?" he scoffed.

Well, I tried.

"No," I smirked. "Because the spirit who came through
for you knows you by a very particular nickname."

Okay, maybe I was enjoying this a little too much. I could

123

tell by the look of horror and surprise on his face that he knew exactly what I was going to say.

"Don't." His eyes widened as his skepticism looked like it had been wiped from his face.

"I believe it was your aunt who called you 'little squish butt' when you were a kid. Does that nickname hold any significance for you?" I lifted my eyebrows knowing full well that he knew the answer to this question. I realized that I might have been going a little too far. But in my defense, he started it!

"Oh God." He looked at my phone, which was streaming this live for half of the school to see. "Not Aunt Ivy."

So, I may have totally embarrassed Stephen to the 280 students that watched my live stream, but to be honest, I didn't exactly feel bad about it after what happened in the cafeteria. Willow said he probably wouldn't live down the whole "squish butt" thing for months, which she felt was the perfect payback for him giving her a mean nickname in elementary school.

By the time I got home, I felt like I was walking on a cloud, and apparently my good mood was obvious enough for even Mom to notice.

"Now that's the smile that I've been missing," Mom said. "You have a good day at school today, honey?"

She'd been in a much better mood ever since we moved out here. She patted the cushion next to her for me to take a seat on our newly upholstered couch. Subtle flower patterns were kind of Mom's whole design aesthetic.

"Guess you could say that." I knew that my definition of a good day and Mom's definition of a good day were not the same thing.

"Yeah, why are you so happy, Paloma?" Magdalena dragged out every word so that her entire sentence sounded like a whine. She was lying on the floor beneath the coffee table. Her eyes twinkled knowingly from the shadows. She couldn't have heard about the live reading. Could she?

"None of your business." She wasn't going to get a confession out of me if that's what she was looking for. "Just made some new friends, that's all."

"That's great, honey," Mom said as she got up to head toward the kitchen. "Your dad's working late at the restaurant tonight, so I need to get dinner started. Hope you're okay with ropa vieja."

Normally that was one of my favorite dishes, but I was

still a little suspicious of Mom's culinary skills after the last time she had tried cooking it. Usually it was either Dad or Abuelito that did all the cooking back home in Miami, so Mom never really had a ton of chances to practice. But since Dad was busy working the late shift at his new job tonight, dinner was up to Mom and I wasn't sure if my stomach was prepared for whatever she was about to concoct. I mean, I get that the dish was called *old clothes* but she didn't need to take it so literally. It actually tasted like I was eating a pair of socks.

In addition to Mom not having psychic abilities from Abuela, she also didn't inherit the cooking gene from Abuelito. Poor Mom. At least she was good with plants.

After dinner, I went into my room to see if I got any more notifications on my social media account and was pleasantly surprised when I had more messages waiting for me than I expected! I combed through them all with a twinge of delight.

@JeremyBearimy123 said I should do this every week and @Omargeddon thought my livestream was the funniest thing he's seen all year!

#Squishbutt was trending.

New supporters kept pouring in as I watched my follower

count go up. I had messages from classmates I'd never even seen asking if they could have a reading. With this many people interested, I was going to have to do more readings. Maybe even two a day! @JeremyBearimy123 would be happy about that. All I needed to do was make sure Mom never found out. That was going to be the hardest part. She always seemed to know what I was up to.

My phone pinged, causing me to jump. The thought of getting caught was already putting me on edge. I looked down and saw that instead of a notification, it was a text from a number I'd never seen before.

UNKNOWN NUMBER: Hey Paloma, it's Thalia. Adding you to the group chat with Fatima and Willow. Can't wait to see you in school tomorrow!

UNKNOWN NUMBER: Great job with the Instagram ghost thing! We crushed it! This is Willow btw

UNKNOWN NUMBER: Go team @TotallyPsychic!

Today couldn't possibly have gone any better. My first successful live reading and new friends to cheer me on! I hoped Abuela would be proud of me too. I sent her a quick note on the spirit mirror to let her know how well things were going since she wanted me to keep her posted. I also wanted to make sure that she knew how much I was improving in case it might help change her mind about taking me on tour. She replied almost immediately.

Such great news, my darling! I'm so glad to hear your first reading was a success. You are well on your way to great things, just like your abuela. Try not to overwork yourself.

Thanks Abuela! I replied. *And don't worry, I won't do anything more than what I can handle.*

We are so proud of you! Another message appeared on the spirit mirror. This time, it wasn't Abuela. I recognized the handwriting from all the years of getting greeting cards for every holiday. It was Aunt Rosa, my cheering squad. The only thing I couldn't figure out was what she was doing in the spirit mirror chat. I thought this was a direct line to Abuela.

As if Abuela knew exactly what I was thinking, she replied.

I forgot to mention I added you to the family group chat, Paloma! That way if you have any questions that I'm not able to answer, the rest of the family will be here to help you!

Always here for you my, sweet niece! Aunt Rosa replied in her extraswirly script.

Have you been keeping your dream journal? I'd love to hear how the new move is manifesting in your unconscious mind! Ugh, Aunt Maria, not now.

Thankfully all of the messages came through in my relatives' handwritings which made it easier to differentiate between each message. Once the topic had changed to discussing baseball scores, I closed the spirit mirror and wondered if they were able to see I've left the conversation. I put the compact back in my bedside drawer beneath Oscar. I gave him a poke on his one eye that looked like it was sliding off to make sure it was still secure.

Right as I was about to drift off to sleep, I realized something terrible: now that the whole family knew about my reading today, there was no way I'd be able to keep this from Mom for long!

11

Lisa's Cat

The next morning, I got up and immediately reached for my notebook. I promised Aunt Maria I would start keeping a dream journal, but the second I opened to a blank page, swirls of flowers began to appear. I quickly grabbed *The Book of Flowers* to decipher them. Marigolds. The symbol for positivity. Laurels for glory and…hellebore, the symbol for overcoming scandal.

That's weird, I thought. I wasn't even trying to do a self-prediction.

By the time I got to school, I could barely sit still in any of my classes. All I could think about was the next reading with Lisa Duncan, who must have been the most talkative girl in school. She had messaged me all night about it.

My phone wouldn't stop pinging until I finally agreed to meet with her right before lunch. I felt sort of bad booking her next because she wasn't even the first person to ask for a reading. She was just the most annoying about it and since I was getting overwhelmed by all of those messages, I agreed to meet with her.

During the first few minutes of lunch, Thalia helped me set up the area in the greenhouse where I would be doing the reading while Willow and Fatima worked on getting the tripod ready. I repositioned some of the hanging flower baskets to give a waterfall effect of ivy as a backdrop and even made sure I had my spirit mirror handy next to my candles in case we were dealing with a non-verbal ghost. I was all set. Though I had a feeling I wouldn't be getting much use out of the spirit mirror if we were dealing with anyone related to Lisa.

Lisa practically skipped into the greenhouse. Her long ponytail bounced along her back with each step and a pink sunburn skated down her white nose. How was she always in such a good mood? It was unsettling. Wasn't she supposed to be grieving someone?

"Oh my gosh, Paloma, I'm so glad you picked me for your next reading!" Her perfectly straight teeth were exposed in a boxy smile. She rocked back and forth in one place like someone who'd chugged way too many energy drinks. "Can't tell you how excited I am to see what kind of ghost wants to talk to me. Like, can you believe it, I'm going to talk to an actual live ghost?"

There was no such thing as a "live" ghost, Lisa. That's why they were ghosts. Everybody knows that.

"Right." I flashed a half grin. "You should probably know that you won't actually be able to speak directly to the spirit that comes through. I have to interpret the messages between the two of you."

"Cool, cool!" Lisa said. "Well however it's done, I'm excited about it. My whole family has always been into this sort of thing…ghosts that is! Not that anyone's ever seen any, but I know my mom loves that really old movie *Ghost*, so I'm sure that has to count for something."

She did not just reference that movie. Let me pretend that didn't happen.

"We should get started." I nodded to Willow who pressed the Go Live button on my phone.

"Greetings, classmates of Sequoia Academy! I have with

132

me here today fellow student, Lisa Duncan." I gestured toward Lisa who was currently spinning in her swivel chair. She had more energy than Magdalena after eating a bowl of ice cream. "We're going to see who comes through for her today."

"Hey all!" Lisa waved to the camera and loudly smacked on her gum. Maybe that was her secret to white teeth.

I closed my eyes and concentrated until I felt the room begin to quiver. I looked around expecting to see one of Lisa's relatives standing behind her, but there was nothing. Huh, I must have done something wrong. I went through the checklist of steps in my mind and couldn't figure it out. The only spirit in the room was Dustin who floated nearby, and I knew he definitely wasn't here for Lisa.

Upon closer inspection, I noticed Dustin was holding a black-and-white ghost cat that I had never seen before.

"Is that your cat?" I called out to him.

"Nope," he tried feebly to contain the creature that was attempting to wriggle loose from his grasp. "It just landed on my lap when you started to do the reading. You think this might be what came through for Lisa?"

"Must be," I said.

This was a first. Out of the many readings I'd seen

Abuela give, I couldn't remember any animals coming through before. I was excited to see how this was going to play out. This must be one special cat.

"Who are you talking to?" Lisa snapped her gum. I was sure that whatever she was chewing had to have run out of flavor by now.

Willow, Fatima, and Thalia looked equally perplexed. They could only hear *my* half of the conversation with Dustin, so I had to fill them in on what was happening. Fatima moved a little closer to me with the boom, making sure to pick up every word.

"Right. Sorry," I said. "Just talking to one of the school ghosts, Dustin. He said a ghost cat landed on his lap. We're trying to figure out if it's connected to you or if it's a stray."

I had no idea if stray ghost cats were even a thing!

"Oreo! Are you telling me my sweet little Oreo came through for me?" Lisa pressed both her hands against her heart. "I can't tell you how happy this makes me. What's he doing right now, can you tell me?"

I didn't think it was physically possible for her smile to get any bigger.

"Um…" I looked over at Dustin who now seemed to be

wearing the cat as a hat. Oreo was arched over his head in a way that could not possibly be comfortable for either one of them.

"Well." I cleared my throat. "It seems Oreo has climbed up the back of Dustin's shirt and is sitting on top of his head. I wish you could see this because it looks pretty ridiculous."

"Oh, Oreo, it really is you!" Lisa pulled out her phone to show me an image of Oreo flopped on top of her head like a furry pair of headphones. "My sweet little Oreo passed away last month. I've been a wreck ever since. Please tell your ghost friend to give him a nice scratch behind his left ear. It's his favorite."

"You got that Dustin?" I called out.

It looked like Oreo and Dustin were really bonding! Oreo nuzzled into the nape of his neck.

"What?" he shouted.

"I love you, Oreo!" Lisa blew a big kiss in the wrong direction. "Thank you so much for this, Paloma, I really mean it. This was so special." She turned to the camera. "Everyone make sure you book time to meet with Paloma, she is the REAL DEAL!"

Wow, that was nice of her! I guess Lisa wasn't so bad after all.

Once we ended the live stream, Lisa gave me the biggest hug and skipped her way back out of the room. So much energy and positivity in one person. I never would have guessed that she had been mourning the loss of her cat all this time. If this was Lisa when she was grieving, I was almost afraid to see what happy Lisa looked like.

Normally at this point, the spirits of the sitter's loved one would disappear after I'd concentrate on sending them back with my candles, but this cat was super stubborn. Oreo was now back on Dustin's shoulder like a big fluffy parrot. I closed my eyes and tried concentrating even harder on sending him back through the portal once again, but nothing happened. The more the cat played with Dustin, the less transparent he was beginning to look. Oreo was here to stay!

"I hope you like cats because it looks like you might have a pet now," I said.

"Fine by me," Dustin said as Oreo rubbed his head against his cheek.

"Wait, so the cat stayed?" Willow jumped up and down in place before handing me back my phone. "That is so

cool, Paloma! We're going to have to update your followers about this! They're going to love it."

"Are you sure you don't mind?" I looked over at Dustin.

"I always wanted a cat," he said, smiling at Oreo. "I was
too allergic to get one before, but this ghost cat seems to
be pretty hypoallergenic. Haven't sneezed yet!"

I let my friends know that Oreo was now happily enjoying his new home in the greenhouse with Dustin. Abuela
was going to love this. I sent her a quick note on the spirit
mirror to give her the update. Maybe once she found out
that I was able to summon ghost animals, she would want
to invite me on tour with her. I bet she'd never heard of
anything like this before!

"Such a great reading!" Fatima said as she began packing up the microphone and tripod. "We have to give the
equipment back to the film department before lunch is
over but we are really on a roll with these!"

"I really appreciate you helping out today," I said. "I don't
know what I would have done without you all!"

"I can't wait until the next one!" Thalia said.

"Oh and Paloma, before I go," Willow said on her way
out the door. "How would you like to come to my birthday party this weekend?"

"A party?" I beamed. "Of course! I'd love to go."

Did this mean I was an official member of the friend group?

"Everyone from school is going to be there." Willow pulled out an envelope from her bag and handed it to me.

I stared at the outside of the card. The words *You're invited* were plastered at the top in a big, bolded font.

You're invited to Willow's Birthday Party Spectacular
Where: Willow's House
When: Saturday, 6:00 p.m.
Theme: Old Hollywood Movies

If everyone from school was going to be there, how could I say no to that?

"Willow's birthday parties are a super big deal around here." Thalia tapped the top of my card with her finger.

"It's true." Fatima nodded. "Her parents go all out with the party planning. You're going to want to be there. It's always the talk of the school for weeks afterward!"

"And because we are such good friends now," Willow said, "you're officially on the VIP list."

"VIP?" My eyes widened as I stared at the invite in my

hands. I couldn't believe I was actually invited to a party. I guess my new friends really did like me after all!

Luckily I didn't have to travel too far for my next class. My earth science teacher was having us do a lab in the greenhouse where we were supposed to examine different soil types to test the PH balances. The room buzzed with excitement and it definitely wasn't for the soil acidity levels. Everyone in class was talking about the cool ghost cat from my reading with Lisa! She'd made sure that word had gotten around that my readings were even better in person and that the live stream didn't do it justice. I was getting more requests for readings than ever before. If there was anyone who didn't see the reading, they managed to hear all about it from Lisa's dramatic retelling.

"Hey, I saw your live stream today! Very cool stuff!" my lab partner said. "I'm Omar by the way. I don't think we officially met. You might know me from my social media handle @Omargeddon!"

"It's so nice to officially meet you in real life, Omar!" Take that Mom, I was making friends! "I know I still owe you a reading during lunch sometime soon."

"I don't actually have a lunch period." Omar rubbed the

back of his neck. "I'm kind of big on taking extracurriculars, so I don't have a ton of free time. But I am in this Drought Intolerant and Resistant Tree Club, or DIRT for short, that meets after school on Mondays. Maybe we could do the reading before the club starts? We usually get a half hour gap between when class ends and the club begins."

"I've actually been meaning to check that club out anyway." I'd heard lots of good things about it thanks to Dustin. "You're going to have to give me the details on that."

"Definitely!" he said. "Always happy to help a fellow plant pal."

"My mom doesn't exactly know that I am doing these readings and she'd be kind of mad about it if she found out," I explained. "So I need to make sure if I'm staying after school that she doesn't find out what I'm really up to."

"Well then it sounds like DIRT will be the perfect cover." He smiled. "I'm glad I was able to recruit a new member."

He was right though. If I was going to get away with doing readings without my parents knowing, then joining DIRT would give me an excuse for staying late. I was so happy my psychic schedule was already starting to fill up. I was going to be as good as Abuela in no time!

I looked at my social media page. Three hundred followers. Way to go, Lisa!

12

Willow's Party

Fatima wasn't kidding when she mentioned Willow's parents went all out for her parties. An assortment of balloons and oversized present boxes the size of small cars peppered her entire lawn. Giant spotlights danced their way across the house in perfect sync to the party music that was playing inside. And since it was old Hollywood themed, there were mannequins of movie stars and director's chairs on the lawn to make it look like a film set. This was definitely epic.

It didn't take much convincing to get Mom to let me go to the party since she was happy I was making friends with anyone who wasn't a ghost.

The other kids from school filed into the house in waves and a small line was beginning to form at the front door. Willow greeted everyone as they entered.

"Welcome to the party!" She hugged each person and placed their gifts on the table beside her.

"I'm so glad you're here, Paloma!" Willow squealed as I walked in the door. Her strawberry blond hair was teased to extend several inches above her head. She was really pulling off the bad Sandy from *Grease* look. "Also, I meant to ask you this earlier, but I thought it would be cool if you did a reading for me sometime tonight. I want to see what ghosts want to visit me for my birthday. I even got a Ouija board and everything! I'm thinking that we can do it after the big scavenger hunt."

"Oh…uhh, I'm not sure we should do this," I gulped. "My family would be super upset if they found out I was using one of those. They're sort of forbidden in my house."

"Oh don't worry, I won't tell your parents or anything like that!" Willow reassured me. "Besides, everyone is sort of expecting to see you summon some ghosts. I kind of told the entire invite list to expect something even bigger and better than what you did for Lisa. I hope that's okay.

It can't be that much different from the readings you did for Lisa and Stephen, can it?"

I tried to force a smile, but I could feel my anxiety levels spiking. She wasn't going to let this go, and I couldn't ruin her whole party. "Anything for the birthday girl."

Was this why she invited me here? As much as I hoped Willow liked me for more than my powers, I couldn't help but doubt a little. Sweat trickled down the back of my neck as I walked into Willow's house to join the rest of the party. I didn't want to disappoint her on her birthday, but Ouija boards were against the rules for a reason. They were especially dangerous since the chances of bad ghosts coming through were even higher than with a normal reading. Bad ghosts were much harder to send back through the spirit portal. Even harder than stubborn cats. But if I said no, would Willow still want to be my friend? As much as I didn't want to go back to eating lunch alone, I wasn't sure if it was worth the risk to have a bunch of evil ghosts following me around.

There was also the slight issue of not having any of my equipment since I wasn't expecting to do a reading tonight. I tried to convince myself it was going to be fine, even though the gnawing feeling in the pit of my stomach said otherwise. I was just going to have to be extra careful. Anyway, I was sure stores wouldn't sell Ouija boards if they were actually dangerous! I was probably just overreacting. They were toys after all, weren't they? Maybe I'd get lucky and nothing would happen.

Once all the guests arrived, we were separated into groups for a scavenger hunt. I was on a team with Willow, Fatima, and Thalia. The VIP list. We spent the next hour wandering around Willow's giant house searching for items on the list of things we were supposed to find.

"What are we looking for again?" Fatima pressed her cheek against the floor, attempting to use her phone's flashlight to see what was under the couch. Willow's parents' couches were pretty low to the ground, so I didn't think she was having any luck.

"I doubt anything could fit under there," I said, trying to save her the effort.

"So far we've found most of the items. There's the monkey's paw made out of puffed rice treats and chocolate that we found in the kitchen, and a figurine of the Maltese falcon," Thalia said, scanning through the checklist.

"There's one problem though. I can't make out the last item on the list because *somebody* got their chocolatey fingers on it." She glanced in my direction.

"Sorry," I wiped my hands on my jeans, trying to hide the evidence. "That monkey's paw was a lot meltier than I thought it would be. Also I kind of maybe thought the list was a napkin."

"Can't we just ask one of the other guests like we do every other year?" Fatima held the list up to a light, trying to make out the words. "Maybe they'll be generous and help the birthday girl out?"

"Not a chance," Willow said. "I don't want to cheat just because it's my birthday. I'm sure everyone else is having the same amount of trouble finding the items on the list as we are. My parents redesigned the game to make it harder."

"No wonder this is taking forever," Fatima groaned as she got up from the floor. "I thought I was just getting bad at this."

"That explains why no one has won yet." Thalia was beginning to get discouraged. "Usually this game is over in a half hour. I feel like we've been doing this all night."

My attempt to clean the chocolate off the list only resulted in spreading it out even further. I eventually gave up and handed it back over to Fatima. She took a photo of the list with her phone and started playing with the contrasts.

"Hey, I think I figured out what this last one says!" Fatima triumphed. "It's…oh. It's a ruby slipper, can that be right?"

"Seriously?" Thalia looked over Fatima's shoulder.

"I might know where to find one." Willow was already on her way up the stairs, confidently walking past several mannequins dressed in old Hollywood costumes, sequined dresses, and feather boas.

The rest of the group followed Willow and ended up inside a hallway closet. A single light bulb attached to a string swayed ominously after Willow shut the door with the three of us inside. I felt my heart jump. We stood in the darkness until someone pulled the cord. The bulb swung back and forth cascading its light from one side of the closet to the other.

I immediately jumped backward the moment the light reached an unexpected figure standing in the room. A man with a scarred face stared back at us. His face went in and out of focus as the light continued its pendulum swing. The shadows drifted across his frame. I realized I was the only one who could see him—he must have been a ghost. I decided not to say anything about it since I didn't want to freak anyone out that Willow had a ghost residing in her upstairs closet.

"It's pretty chilly in here, isn't it?" Willow rubbed her arms. "I wonder where that draft could be coming from."

I pretended to look under a few towels in an attempt to forget about the ghost standing next to me. He was eerily still.

"Willow's parents like to hide these things in places we wouldn't think to look," Fatima said. "There was one year we won by default because everyone else forfeited."

"That was a good year," Thalia agreed. "You know what they say, the best competition is no competition."

"I don't think anyone says that," Fatima argued.

"I just know I have an old bin of shoes in here some-where." Willow rummaged through boxes of old summer clothes and photo albums. "Huh," she paused. "I could have sworn I saw it recently. I know I have a pair of red slippers in there."

"Her parents moved it for the scavenger hunt," a deep gravelly voice boomed.

But the lips of the ghost standing near the light bulb didn't move. The sound was coming from a sleepy-looking ghost with deep bags under his eyes who was lounging on a pile of folded bedding on the top shelf. So, there were two ghosts in the room. Great.

"Oh, uh…" I looked skeptically at the ghost. "Thanks for the tip?"

"Paloma, who are you talking to?" Thalia knit her brow in confusion.

"Oh God, is there a ghost in here?" Fatima exclaimed as she reached for the door. "That's it, I'm out."

"Fatima, come back!" Willow shouted.

"Eh, she'll get over it." Thalia peeked her head out of the door to check on Fatima who was now sitting at the top of the stairs.

"So, what did the ghost say?" Willow scanned the room trying to find the source of information. "Does it know where the slippers are?"

The ghost now appeared to be napping again.

"Uh, sort of. The ghost just mentioned your parents took

the box out of here for the scavenger hunt," I said, then turned my attention back to the top shelf of the closet. "Do you know where they took the box?"

"No idea," the ghost opened one eye and replied with an agitated tone. "Now do you mind turning off the light when you leave? Some people are trying to sleep here."

"What about you?" I asked the ghost standing by the light bulb who was still scowling at my friends.

"No," he grumbled.

"Right. Sorry for disturbing you both!" I left the room, making sure to turn off the light on my way out.

Once we were back in the hallway, Willow pulled me aside from the rest of the group.

"So?" Willow whispered in case any of our competitors were lurking nearby. "Do we know where to look?"

"It doesn't seem like these ghosts get out too much." I shook my head. "They have no idea where the box went, just that it left that room. Sorry for the dead end."

A loud cheer came from downstairs. Someone must have found all the items on the list.

"Darn, I hate losing." Thalia fidgeted with a hallway drawer handle.

The four of us descended the stairs until we rejoined the rest of the party who were gathered in the living room.

"I found it. I found it!" Lisa Duncan waved the small red shoe above her head as the rest of the room cheered and applauded.

Did she really need to rub it in? Whatever, Lisa.

"Well, I guess I can't win every year." Willow shrugged and joined in on the clapping. "Congrats, Lisa!"

She walked over and handed Lisa a giant pin that said Scavenger Champ.

"You earned it!" Willow said, giving her the biggest hug.

"Where'd you find the last item anyway?" Fatima asked once the cheers subsided. "I feel like I looked everywhere for that slipper."

"Under the couch." Lisa pointed to the same couch that Fatima had been inspecting earlier. The same one I had told her to stop looking under. Whoops.

"Darn it, I looked there." Fatima pouted as she crossed her arms, taking a seat on the couch that had betrayed her. She looked pretty upset—I hoped she wasn't mad at me.

"So, what next?" One of the other party guests asked.

I recognized them as one of the students from my Spanish class.

"I think it's time we summon some ghosts!" Willow looked in my direction and I instantly felt my heart race. Part of me hoped that she would have forgotten about the Ouija board. Every single person at the party turned to me with excitement in their eyes, but no one looked more eager than Willow. How could I say no after everything she'd done to help me?

"I guess one reading couldn't hurt," I said, trying to sound more confident than I felt. There was no backing out now.

Willow pulled out a Ouija board from the living room cabinet. It looked harmless enough.

"Yay, Paloma," Lisa cheered. "This is going to be great!"

Not helping, Lisa! She obviously didn't realize that this was going to be different than the reading I had done for her. My insides knotted up. Maybe I could stall! I needed to give myself some time to think of how I could get out of this!

"The name *Ouija* comes from the French and German words for yes, and although it is used as a game today, it kind of fell out of fashion because there was no controlling what kind of ghosts would appear, so we are going to be taking our chances tonight by using this," I said. Especially since I didn't have my candles. But I didn't say that part out loud.

"We're not here for a history lesson!" someone shouted.

Well, that was rude. I spread out the board on the table and felt the eyes of everyone in the room watching my every move.

Willow sat across from me on the floor, beaming with excitement. Begonias popped out of her tall, teased hair. The flower for caution. That definitely wasn't making me feel any better.

"Maybe we shouldn't do this," I whispered to Willow. "I'm getting some bad…vibes."

The room was loud with the chatter of the other party-goers.

"What?" Willow strained to hear me and pointed to the board. "Just press down on the little heart-shaped plastic thing."

"Okay," I inhaled deeply and placed my hand on top of the planchette. "Here goes nothing."

The second Willow placed her hands on top of mine, the

planchette zoomed across the board to spell the word *hello*. At least we were working with a friendly ghost. I hoped that a bad ghost wouldn't be this polite. The crowd standing around us "ooo'd and ahh'd" as the device freely moved across the board. I decided if I was already doing this, I might as well make it a little more interesting. I swayed my body with each movement of the planchette for dramatic effect.

I was so caught up in the theatrics of it all that I didn't notice right away that there was a disembodied hand on top of mine and Willow's as we were spelling words. I shuddered. The hand was frail and boney, with large bulging veins wrapped around each finger like snakes. It was clear this hand belonged to an elderly individual. The relationship to Willow was still unknown. It took a few more minutes before the rest of the spirit came into focus.

"Birthday girl! The spirit spelled birthday girl! It knows it's my birthday!" Willow clapped her hands. "Oh isn't this so much fun, Paloma! Do you know who the spirit is? Obviously its someone who knows it's my birthday."

The sash and tiara she was wearing that said birthday girl on it could have also been a giveaway. This might not even be someone who knew her at all.

"I'm not sure who the spirit is yet or how they are connected to you, but that can be one of the questions we ask them," I said.

"Yes!" Willow sat up a little straighter and put her own hands on the planchette. "I would like to know who is wishing me a happy birthday."

Her cheeks were still red from smiling. Maybe breaking the rules was worth it to make my new friend feel this happy. I'm sure Abuela would understand.

The shuttle zoomed again across the board in a forceful motion to spell the word *Grandpa*. The hand and the rest of the spirit's form disappeared as soon as the shuttle reached the final *a*.

"It looks like your grandpa came through to wish you a happy birthday," I said, making sure to project loudly so that the rest of the room could hear, just like Abuela would have. A few of the partygoers had been crowding around a little closer to get a good look at the board, which blocked the view for everyone else, so I made sure to relay everything that was going on for anyone who couldn't see.

I wondered where Willow's grandpa disappeared to.

Could he have just crossed back over on his own? In a swoop of panic, I realized that I had no idea how to close a spirit portal without my candles.

This wasn't good.

"Thank you so much, Paloma," Willow said. "Best birthday present ever. This was so much fun. Now who wants dessert?!"

Everyone in the room threw their hands up and ran toward the kitchen. Willow and I stayed behind to put the board back in the cabinet.

"Thank you again for doing the reading," Willow said once everyone had left. "It really means a lot to me that my grandpa came to visit."

"Of course!" I hoped she couldn't tell how anxious I had been during the whole thing. Part of me was still stressing out that something was going to go horribly wrong.

Stop worrying over nothing, I scolded myself. *Everything is fine.*

Yet, I couldn't shake the fear that summoning ghosts was the only reason why I was invited to the party in the first place. I could only hope that wasn't the case.

By the end of the night, there were six of us left at the party who were staying for the sleepover. This was the VIP list that Willow had been talking about, including myself, Thalia, Fatima, Lisa, Heather from Spanish class, and Willow's cousin, Ruth.

"Do you think we can use the Ouija board again, Paloma?" Willow asked.

She had changed into her matching pajama set, her hair now compressed against her head and pulled back into a tight ponytail. No more 1980s big hair.

"I don't think we should," I said.

I didn't exactly want to tempt fate twice, even if nothing bad had happened the first time. I wasn't ready to take that chance. Those boards could be finicky. Plus, I still couldn't figure out how the ghosts disappeared without me using the candles to close the portal.

All of Abuela's warnings ran through my head. There was one story in particular that she always told about a relative who used a Ouija board and got trapped in the spirit world forever. I shuddered at the thought. I couldn't sleep for days after the first time I'd heard that one. Aunt Maria reassured me that it was just a story and that Abuela liked to scare us so we wouldn't go breaking the rules. Part of me still wondered if it was true.

Wasn't getting my new friends to like me more important than getting sucked into an alternate dimension forever? Probably.

"It was so fun when you did it before," Heather said.

"Come on, Paloma," Lisa Duncan pleaded. "Just one more time."

I resisted the urge to throw the board at Lisa.

"Alright," I said. "Let's do it."

As soon as I grabbed the Ouija board, ghosts started to flicker in and out of view as even more disembodied limbs wandered around the room. There were so many of them that I was beginning to lose count. Besides that, nothing unusual happened. It seemed like all these boards could do were weaker versions of spirit readings. You couldn't even manifest a full ghost! When I channeled the spirits in the way that Abuela taught me, there were never random pieces of spirits floating around. How was I supposed to communicate with a foot?

We continued summoning spirits for hours, until we were finally tired enough to go to bed. Thankfully none of these spirits had enough energy to write in full sentences, so eventually everyone got bored of the one-word responses. Having to spell everything out took up more energy, so the spirits had to keep their messages short and sweet.

Even though nothing bad happened, I couldn't say I was super interested in doing more Ouija board readings in the future. Traditional readings were much better!

The party was a success, my new friends were happy, and my readings went well. Everything was good. I buried myself deep into the supersoft plushy sleeping bag, took off my glasses, and began to drift off to sleep.

That is, until I heard the sound of my name being called from a distance.

"Paloma," the loud whisper called out.

My eyes sprang open as I was startled into alertness. The voice didn't belong to anyone that I recognized. Who would need to talk to me in the middle of the night? I closed my eyes, tighter this time, hoping that I was hearing things. That it was just a dream. But the second I began to drift back off to sleep again, I heard my name called once more.

"Paloma," the voice said. Louder this time. "I need to talk to you."

Couldn't this wait?

I sat up straight and looked around the room, which didn't do much good considering it was dark and I hadn't put my glassed on yet. All I could make out were the vague amorphous shapes of the other girls who were all still sleeping. But I squinted harder, scanning through the darkness as my eyes began to adjust. There, in the corner of the room, I spotted the faint shadow of a man's figure gliding out the door.

13

Big Secret

"Paloma," the voice called once more. Smaller this time. Farther away.

"It's the middle of the night," I said in my groggy half-asleep stupor. "Can't this wait until the morning?"

"It's important." The voice wavered with a gravelly tremor. It sounded like it belonged to an older man.

Maybe it wasn't a ghost, I reassured myself. This could be one of those lucid dreams that Aunt Maria was always talking about. I was sure there had to be a very reasonable explanation for all of this.

There was only one way to find out, so I rolled off my cot and made my way through the maze of sleeping girls. I slid my feet carefully across the rough carpeting to feel where I was going, making adjustments every time I bumped into something. I searched for the door frame with my arms outstretched in front of my face as I made my way closer toward the sound.

"Please don't be a ghost, please let me be imagining things, please don't be a ghost," I muttered to myself in the hopes that if I said it enough times, it might actually be true. I had a sinking feeling that this had something to do with me using the Ouija board.

Once I was fully out of the room, I turned on my phone's flashlight to see better. Two cold sunken eyes stared back at me, set in a pale translucent face. There was no mistaking that this was a ghost. And not just any ghost, it was Willow's grandfather from earlier today. His deep wrinkles outlined his expression which was cast in a frown. I was surprised he had the energy to cross over twice in one day. Unless… Oh no, unless he never left after the reading. What if that meant none of the other spirits left too?

This was a problem. Without my candles, I had no way of sending him back. So much for my wishful thinking that all of the ghosts would just cross back over on their own. I'd never closed the portal to the spirit world without candles before and I'd never seen Abuela do it either. This was a disaster. I never should have used the Ouija board.

Before this moment, I could confidently say that ghosts didn't scare me, but seeing Willow's grandpa in the middle of the night made my skin crawl.

"What are you still doing here?" I watched my breath leave my mouth. It was a lot colder than usual. I rubbed my arms to try and warm myself up. Willow's grandpa must be pretty powerful!

"I need to tell Willow something urgently," he said. "And I know you're the only one who can help me do that."

"If you'd like, we could do a reading tomorrow and you can talk to her then," I suggested. Why does it have to be now?

"Time is of the essence," he demanded.

"I'm not going to wake her up." I pointed to the window to prove to the ghost that it was still dark out. "Can you at least tell me what this is about? If I'm going to be translating for you anyway, you may as well just tell me what you want to talk to her about, and if it's that urgent than maybe I'll wake her up."

Willow's grandfather glided closer to me.

"Willow's parents are getting divorced, and I want you

to help me stop it." He placed his cold boney hand on my shoulder, which caused me to shiver.

I could hear Abuela's voice in my head reciting the rules of mediumship. Rule number four, "Don't repeat everything a spirit tells you," and rule number five, "Readings should be healing not hurtful." And if we're counting the rule about not forcing contact with the spirits, I would be breaking three rules in one night if I relayed this message. Breaking one rule was enough in my opinion!

Even though this wasn't technically a reading, I felt like the rules still applied. This would definitely fall into the category of not repeating things that might be upsetting. It was exactly the kind of thing that Abuela would tell me I shouldn't be interfering with. I took a step back toward the room with the other girls. Going against the rules already got me into this mess, I wasn't going to break even more to get out of it.

"I'm sorry, I can't help you." I shivered.

How was this one ghost making the room this cold?

"You need to talk to Willow." I could see my reflection staring back at me in his icy stare. "Tell her what's going on. She can put a stop to it."

If Willow's parents wanted to get divorced, I wasn't sure

there was anything I, or Willow, could do to stop it. This was pointless.

"I'm leaving," I said as I maneuvered around another ghost. Wait…what was another ghost doing here?

I felt along the wall for the light switch and flipped it to the on position. Turned out it wasn't just one ghost staring back at me—it was a roomful of ghosts! And way more than what I summoned with the Ouija board, even though it was hard to tell with all those limbs how many ghosts there actually were.

This could only mean one thing: the portal was still open.

I needed to figure out how I was going to send them all back before the rest of the slumber party members woke up. This was going to be extra tricky without my candles. I wasn't even totally sure that it could even be done, but I couldn't let Willow know that I accidentally ripped open a hole to the spirit world in the middle of her house. She would never want to stay friends with me after that. I would officially be off the VIP list for good.

A loud thud came from upstairs. I ran up to investigate only to find even more ghosts causing mischief and pulling books off the shelves.

I needed to come up with a plan. Ideally one that didn't involve Abuela or Mom finding out about this.

Maybe there was something in *The Book of Flowers* about returning ghosts to the spirit world without candles?

I went back to the basement where everyone was sleeping, completely unaware to what was going on in the rest of the house, and grabbed my bag, which thankfully still had the book in it. I skimmed through the pages, desperately scanning the margins for notes from my ancestors. There had to be something in there about spectral emergencies or returning ghosts back to the other side. At least I'd hoped so.

I stopped on a page that had the word *portal* underlined three times. This had to be something!

It read:

Portals are not easy to see, so the best way to locate one is by feel. They are usually in the place with the coldest temperature.

At least this was a start! Though there didn't seem to be any clues about actually closing the portal.

I hated to admit it, but I was going to have to ask for help if I was going to figure out how to send the spirits back, which meant letting my family know I messed up. Unless… I thought for a moment. There was one relative who might be able to help me, and if I played this right, I wouldn't even have to tell them what I did!

Aunt Maria was usually up late anyway to deal with her client's dream problems, so it wouldn't be unusual for me to message her in the middle of the night with a dream problem of my own! She didn't need to know it was an *actual* problem. I could just pass this off like I was having a super vivid nightmare.

I pulled my spirit mirror out of my pocket and began dictating.

Aunt Maria, I had a nightmare about opening a portal to the spirit world by using a Ouija board. If this were to actually happen, how would you recommend closing it? Can it be done without candles? I don't think I'll be able to go back to sleep without knowing!

Maybe I was overselling it a little, but I hoped that sounded convincing. Within seconds, I got a response. Thank goodness one of my relatives was a night owl.

Closing a spirit portal without candles includes deep mediation and a little prayer. It's always easier with candles, but if you don't have any handy, it can still be done if you concen-

trate hard enough. *You need to make sure that if there are ghosts on the loose that you find them all first. Ghosts can end up in a lot of obscure places like under sinks or in cabinets. You sure you said this was a dream?*

Oh no, she was on to me! I needed to throw her off the trail!

Yup! Just one of those lucid dreams you're always telling me about! Thanks!

That should do the trick. She loved lucid dreams.

Another message from Aunt Maria came in. *You do know you really shouldn't mess with those Ouija boards. They lead to all kinds of problems. Even if you close this portal, new ones can pop up in different places if you don't locate all of the spirits that got loose. Portals turn up wherever the spirits go, so be careful. The only way to really make sure it's closed is to use your candles.*

My palms had been sweating so much that I nearly dropped the spirit mirror on the floor.

At least Aunt Maria was right that locating the portal was the easy part. I walked around the house and found the spot with the near arctic temperature pretty quickly. Unsurprisingly, it was in the upstairs closet where the creepy ghost standing behind the light bulb was hanging out.

Now it was time to round up the ghosts, which was going to be a lot harder than any scavenger hunt. It seemed like every place I looked had a ghost hiding and not all of them were willing to leave. I had to use a little bit of trickery to convince them to go upstairs. I told them that there was "something really interesting" that they should go check out in the closet. Once they got close enough to the portal, they disappeared.

After two hours of searching every inch of Willow's house, I felt confident that I had gotten all of the spirits safely out. I even found one that tried hiding behind a toilet tank! Aunt Maria was right about ghosts being in unexpected places.

Now that I had solved the ghost problem, all I could think about was what I was going to tell Willow. Should I tell her about her parents' divorce, like her grandfather wanted? Or should I not tell her anything at all and let her be devastated by the news when it actually happened?

I debated with myself over which was the right thing to do. Do you tell someone the truth about the future and break their heart now...or wait and let them experience it?

Whatever I ended up choosing, I definitely was never telling Willow about the ghost infestation in her upstairs closet or that it was my fault there was an open spirit portal in her house.

By the time I crawled back into my sleeping bag, the sun was already starting to come up and the rest of the girls were beginning to stir. So much for getting a good night's sleep. I felt like a ghost myself, going through the motions of getting dressed and having breakfast. One minute I was dipping my spoon into my bowl of oatmeal, and the next, I was lying face first in it. I picked my head up and started to wipe some of the goopy bits out of my hair, face flaming in embarrassment.

"Hey, Paloma." Thalia waved her hand in front of my face. "Are you with us?"

"Sorry." I did my best impersonation of a fully awake person. "What's up?"

"I think your mom's outside to pick you up. She drives that flower truck, right?" Fatima gestured toward the window.

Her hair was wrapped up in the silk turban that she had slept in last night. It reminded me of the one Suzanne La Luca had been wearing on the night of her reading with

Abuela. No wonder her hair always looked so shiny. Mine was still tied back in a mangled braid with frizzy strands popping out from each plait.

"Yeah, that's her," I said, my voice cracking from exhaustion. I could see the Flor's Flower logo on the truck parked outside.

"Did you not sleep last night?" Willow asked.

She had to know the answer to that question since I was face-deep in my breakfast moments earlier.

"I slept great!" Lisa said. "Those cots were surprisingly comfortable."

Nobody asked you, Lisa!

"I'm just not a morning person," I lied. "Anyway, thank you so much for having me, Willow! This was super fun."

Once I was back home, I zombie walked down the hall, past Magdalena doing handstands next to her lizard tank—she practically carried that thing with her everywhere at this point—and I flopped on my bed.

A few hours later, I woke up feeling, well, not refreshed, but at least I was a bit more awake. I felt a pang of sympathy for all the times I'd heard dad grumble about needing his morning café con leche. There was nothing quite like Cuban coffee to pack a punch. Or so he said.

171

Beryl was in the living room waiting to greet me as soon as I had gotten up from my nap. She was sitting on the couch surrounded by the large pile of pillows.

"What are you doing in there?" I asked.

"Trying to hide from all those ghosts outside," Beryl replied. She was currently sandwiched between two couch cushions that made it look like she was being engulfed. "Our neighborhood sure has gotten a lot noisier lately."

I looked out the window to see that Beryl was right, there was *a lot* more spirit activity than usual. The group of skateboarding ghosts grew to an uncountable number, there were ghosts going for walks, and even ghosts driving phantom cars. There were ghosts literally everywhere!

This couldn't be because of me, could it?

"I'm sure they're just passing through." My voice wavered.

Before Beryl could reply, I felt my phone buzz in my pocket. It was Jasmin and Keisha. At least that was something to get my mind off of this potential ghost problem.

"Hey!" I said after accepting their video call. "How are you two doing?"

"You mean three!" Jasmin corrected. "Eloise is here too,

she's just off in the other room. We were hoping she would come by to say hi, so you two can officially meet!"

I still couldn't believe they had a new best friend already. I guess I was easily replaceable.

"We were just calling to see how things were going since we haven't heard from you in a couple of days," Keisha said.

"Actually, things haven't been super great." I made sure to move our conversation out of the living room so that I was out of earshot from Mom and Magdalena. I couldn't risk them hearing my confessional about what happened last night.

I told them both the whole story of how I accidentally ripped open a portal to the spirit world, unleashing dozens of ghosts into Willow's house in the middle of the night, almost ruining her entire party.

"Whoa," Jasmin said. "Sounds like things got out of hand over there."

"See, that's what happens when you don't have us around to help you stay out of trouble." Keisha smiled.

"Well, the good news is, I think I was able to fix the portal problem. The bad news is Willow's grandpa was so insistent that I tell her about some super private family stuff and now I feel like I know information about her parents that I shouldn't," I added.

"Hmm, that does sound like a tricky situation to be in, but I'm glad you were able to fix the portal thing at least," Keisha said. "And I agree, it's not great to know information that you don't want to know about someone's family secret. What are you planning to tell Willow?"

"I haven't figured that part out yet," I said. "I think right now I am leaning toward not telling her because I don't want to make her upset. The other thing is, the reason why this whole mess happened in the first place was because Willow really wanted me to use the Ouija board even though I told her I didn't want to, and now I'm worried that she only invited me to the party so I could use my powers."

"Don't meddle with family secrets." Jasmin shook her head. "That's just going to cause problems. Also, from what it sounds like, Willow is a good friend. Isn't she even helping with your readings at school?"

"Agreed," Keisha said. "That info should come from her parents, not from you. Her grandpa was asking way too much of you in that situation. And you do know you are way more than your powers, right? Willow probably thought it would be a fun idea to do a séance at the party. Besides, anyone can use a Ouija board. You don't need to have powers for that."

Even though I knew deep down that they were right, I still couldn't help but feel stressed about the whole thing. It was going to be so weird to see Willow at school tomorrow, knowing that I had to keep such a big secret from her. A secret that I shouldn't even know!

"I guess I shouldn't get too paranoid about these things," I sighed. "Thank you for always being such good listeners."

"That's what friends are for," Keisha said. "It's good to be open to new friends coming into your life. It's kind of like how we were so lucky to find Eloise after you moved."

"You're right," I said, ignoring the part about Eloise.

"Of course," Jasmin said. "We're always here for you."

14

Phantom Food Fight

The anxiety of what happened at Willow's party was starting to get to me and my powers were seriously on the fritz. Stress and psychic abilities did not mix well. The rest of the weekend, I kept seeing flowers popping out of everything, not just people. There were tansies, the flower for hostility, coming out of my dresser, begonias, the symbol for caution sprouting from my lamp, and even yellow carnations, the symbol for disappointment descending from my ceiling.

When my alarm went off Monday morning, I wrapped myself tighter in my blankets, not wanting to move from my bed. After my call with Jasmin and Keisha, I still couldn't decide whether or not I should tell Willow the message from her grandpa just so that I could get this secret off my chest. I didn't know how much longer I could keep this bottled up. I felt like a dormant volcano that was about to awaken and explode at any second. I looked down into the face of my botanical bestie, Oscar, for some guidance, but his plastic pupils rocked toward the floor, avoiding my gaze.

When I got on the school bus, I realized something else was seriously off. There were even more ghosts around than there were yesterday. It was as if all the ghosts that Beryl had been hiding from last night were now on my bus. Seeing a few ghosts floating around in different places was normal, but seeing this many ghosts in one place meant that something was very wrong. Like a portal still being open to the spirit world kind of wrong.

But this couldn't be my fault. Could it? I closed the portal at Willow's house. At least I thought I had. I followed Aunt Maria's directions and everything *seemed* fine when I did it.

Then I remembered what Aunt Maria said. If I didn't send all of the ghosts back through the portal, another one could open up somewhere else. Could that be what was happening? This new portal could be anywhere—how on earth was I supposed to find it? I felt my entire body going into panic mode. Even my stress hives were back.

Now I had two problems I needed to solve today: avoiding Willow in case I accidentally said anything about her parents, and figuring out what was going on with all these ghosts. Also, I was also pretty sure I had a quiz in my Spanish class that I was not prepared for. So that was three problems.

This was going to be a long day.

The bus sounded like total chaos with all of the ghosts trying to talk over each other. I put in my earbuds and turned the volume all the way up in an attempt to try to drown out the noise. I needed to find the spirit portal where these ghosts were coming from and get them out of here. And I needed to do it fast.

My jaw nearly dropped when we pulled up to the school. The entire front lawn looked like a festival of ghosts from every era possible. There were flapper ghosts and sixties hippie ghosts and ghosts in outfits that I had never even seen before heading straight for the school!

Well, at least I was now pretty certain that I figured out

where the spirit portal was, my school. With this much ghost activity, it had to be around here somewhere.

I clutched my backpack protectively to my chest and walked straight into the building. A chill passed over me with every ghost I walked near. I did my best to avoid walking through them, but with this many, it was pretty hard to avoid them all. Walking through a ghost was a very unpleasant experience. I made the mistake of doing it once, and I've successfully avoided it ever since…until now. It was kind of like taking a cold shower, if the water was made out of slime. This was total ghost overload. If there was ever a time to be wearing a sweater, it was now. Every hair on my body was standing on end.

I didn't think I'd ever been this happy to see Barry in my life. He stood at the front entrance of the school making an effort to keep hundreds of ghosts from flooding into the building. Go Barry!

"Alright, anyone who is not a student must exit the premise immediately." He escorted a pair of women in poodle skirts down the stairs of the entrance.

"Barry, you're amazing." I'd hug him if I could.

"No time for hellos." Barry was distracted by another set of ghosts attempting to enter the building. "You need to get to class before you're late. I'll work on keeping these ghosts out of here. Vete ya! THIS IS PRIVATE SCHOOL PROPERTY. STUDENTS AND FACULTY ONLY!"

He charged toward the front door. It really felt like this was the moment of Barry's career that he had been waiting for.

I got to my first class and felt a wave of relief that everyone in the room was living. Interacting with too many ghosts at once was a major battery drainer for mediums and I needed to conserve my energy for closing the portal.

I waved at Willow, but my face immediately dropped when I saw several ghosts sneak in behind her. They must have gotten past Barry. And to make things even worse, Willow's grandfather was here.

"Did you tell her yet?" he whispered before disappearing into a crowd of spirits.

"No, no, no, no, no, no." I covered my ears as I slinked further into my chair. I could barely hear my own thoughts over the loud chatter from the group of ghosts. If Willow's grandfather was here, that meant he was able to find his way through the new portal that opened in the school.

"Well, it's nice to see you too." A confused look was plastered onto Willow's face.

"Oh, sorry!" My body slumped in the chair. "There's just a lot of spirits in the room right now and it's a little overwhelming."

"That sounds stressful," Willow said. "Is there anything I can do to help?"

"Not really." I frowned. "I just have figure out where all the ghosts are coming from so I can send them all back."

I left out the part that this was all the result of using the Ouija board since I didn't want her to feel bad that this whole thing was kind of partly her fault.

"Well if you need any help, count me in," she said, taking a seat next to me. "And I'm sure Thalia and Fatima would be more than willing to as well."

It was nice to hear that I wouldn't have to deal with this alone. Maybe I could use their help after all!

I remembered what *The Book of Flowers* said about the temperature drop near the portal. You didn't have to be a medium to be able to locate a spirit portal. Anyone could feel the sudden temperature change. Non-mediums always reacted to the chill that came from a ghost entering the room. This would be the same thing but on a larger scale. If we all split up and searched to school for cold spots, we could cover more ground and find the portal even faster!

"Meet me in our usual spot during lunch," I said. "I think I know how you can help track down the spirit portal."

"You got it," Willow said.

My next few classes were sadly not ghost-free either. There were sword-fighting ghosts and pirate ghosts fighting each other on top of my teacher's desk. And lunch was even worse. Instead of the chaotic sounds of cafeteria chatter, I walked into a full-out brawl of teenage ghosts having a spectral food fight in the air. Dustin was caught in the crossfire and his rugby shirt was now dotted with globs of ectoplasmic food. Half of a glowing banana peel hung on his shoulder and Oreo was licking whatever goo was stuck to Dustin's hair. He looked even more stressed-out than I did.

The table that Willow, Fatima, and Thalia usually sat at was now occupied by a Girl Scout troop selling ghost cookies. I told my friends what was going on and how we needed to find the spirit portal in order to send these ghosts back to wherever they came from.

"At least that explains why it's so chilly in here today." Thalia zipped up her hoodie. "Although I don't love knowing that I have just been standing next to creepy ghosts all day."

One of the Girl Scouts was visibly offended by that comment and attempted to stomp on Thalia's foot.

"I'm afraid so," I said.

"Let's get these ghosts out of here." Fatima rubbed her arms to stay warm. "I need this temperature to go back to normal. I don't think I could deal with another day of this cold."

"I'm sure between the four of us, we will find this portal in no time!" Willow clapped her hands together.

I was glad for Willow's optimism because I was not feeling as confident. This school was huge.

"If you think it's cold now, just know that the spot near the spirit portal is ten times colder. That's how you'll be able to tell when you're close," I said. "Trust me."

"Have you done this sort of thing before?" Willow asked.

"No, I uh…" I paused to think of an answer that didn't involve mentioning her party. "I just read about them."

The first stop on my search for the portal was in the auditorium. Turned out it was the only room in the school that was suspiciously ghost-free. And it looked like Barry was trying to keep it that way. Apparently, most of the ghosts were too afraid of Lucy Lammermoor to impede on her turf. Barry barricaded himself against the auditorium doors to hold back any potential unwanted guests just in case, but he made an exception for Dustin, who arrived after he finally got away from that food fight.

Dustin perched himself on a tall ladder on the stage to put some distance between himself and Lucy, who had been scolding him for having poor posture. At least this was still better than having phantom spaghetti thrown at your head.

"I'm not sure I can hold this door back much longer." Barry was looking more transparent than ever. His strength was fading fast since he was using all of his energy to keep the spirits from passing through the walls.

"I thought no one wanted to come in here because they were all too afraid of Lucy," I said.

"You're forgetting the one group of ghosts that aren't afraid of her." Dustin descended the ladder with Oreo wrapped around his neck like a furry ascot.

"What group would that be?" I asked.

"Theatre kids." He floated out of the room seconds before Barry's hold on the door lapsed.

"There's too many of 'em," Barry said before a flood of ghosts started passing through into the room.

I headed for the exit right as Barry toppled over. A hundred chorus students singing Sondheim made their way toward the stage. Lucy Lammermoor had never looked happier, her arms outstretched to welcome her students.

I met up with my friends before the bell rang for our next class. I already determined the spirit portal wasn't in the auditorium since the room was absent of the arctic cold chill that I had felt at Willow's house.

So far, none of us had any luck locating the portal. Willow checked all the locker rooms, Thalia searched the greenhouse, and Fatima went looking in the basement since she figured that would probably be the scariest spot in the school and therefore the most likely to have a spirit portal. But none of these locations had the drastic temperature change we were looking for. We agreed to resume our search after school. Aunt Maria did say that portals and ghosts were often in the places we least expected.

The ghost situation however continued to get worse with each passing minute. My earth science class was filled with newspaper boys reading outdated headlines. And on top of that, my powers started freaking out againn. Yellow carnations were appearing everywhere. As if things couldn't keep getting worse, I saw something that really made my heart sink. It was Willow's grandpa again, and this time he was heading straight for me!

"Have you told her yet?" He hovered over my desk.

I groaned and covered my face, hoping he would disappear. His persistence was really starting to get annoying.

"Do you need to go to the nurse?" Omar leaned over to ask. "You don't look so good."

"I'm fine," I whispered back, willing it to be true.

Then again, if I left to go to the nurse, that would give me the chance to keep searching for the portal!

"Actually, I should probably go." I grabbed my stomach, pretending to be sick.

I flung myself out of my desk and ran for the door. I was almost on my way to freedom when I heard Mr. Schubert's deep baritone voice cut through the noise.

"Where do you think you're going, young lady? I didn't excuse you." I could feel the eyes of my whole class looking at me. "We don't knock over desks in this classroom."

I looked back at my desk which was toppled over on the floor. I must have gotten up more forcefully than I realized.

"Going to the nurse!" I shouted. "Stomach ache!"

I ran out of the room before he could even reply.

The hallways were filled with the ghosts that Barry had tried so hard to keep out. Poor Barry. He'd done his best.

The hall was so packed that it was hard to tell who was a student and who was a ghost. The only way to differentiate was the fact that the ghosts were wearing outfits from bygone eras, and the students were shivering and rubbing their arms due to the cold. Thankfully ghosts weren't the first thing that came to mind when someone felt a little chilly. Hopefully my classmates just thought there was something wrong with the school's air-conditioning system and not that I accidentally unleashed ghosts in the school. The guilt I felt was overwhelming.

I wandered around every inch of the school trying to find the cold spot and sent a quick text to my friends to keep them updated on where I had already looked.

ME: Anyone find the portal entrance yet?

WILLOW: Nope. But I can look some more in between classes

FATIMA: Same. And I'm still down to search with you all after school if we don't find it by then

THALIA: Sounds like a plan

When I got to Spanish class, it was time for me to face my third problem of the day. The quiz that I didn't study for.

"Ready for the quiz?" Heather asked. She tapped her pencil nervously against her desk.

I frowned and shook my head as soon as I saw Señora Santos passing around our exams.

"Not at all," I said.

From what I could tell, Heather was pretty good at Spanish. I, on the other hand, was not. You would think growing up in a bilingual household would have rubbed off, but sadly not! My Spanish speaking skills were about as good as my ability to close spirit portals.

After taking the quiz that I was pretty sure I failed, I met up with Willow, Fatima, and Thalia by the greenhouse. I let Mom know that I would be home late because I needed to study. I couldn't tell her that I had gone against the rules and used a Ouija board, causing the spirit portal to open up in my school and that now I was dealing with hundreds of spirits following me around everywhere. I'd be grounded for life!

Once we were all in the greenhouse, my friends and I drew out a map of the school and circled all of the places we already looked.

"Are you positive it's in the school?" Willow asked. "I think we've looked everywhere at this point."

"I mean, it has to be." I paused. "There wouldn't be this much spirit activity here otherwise."

The Book of Flowers said that spirits usually didn't wander too far from portal openings since it was a source of energy for them, so it had to be in the school.

"Okay, well if it's in the school," Thalia said, "it looks like the only two places we haven't looked are the gym and the cafeteria. Should we split up again like we did before?"

"But we were in the cafeteria during lunch," Fatima pointed out.

"Yes, but we didn't actually look there," Thalia argued. She had a point.

"Let's stick together this time," I said. "We already covered a lot of ground today, and we only have a couple of more places to look. I'm hoping we'll have a better chance finding it now."

"Need any extra help?" Dustin floated behind my group of friends with Oreo perched on his shoulder.

"Always. We can use all the help we can get," I replied.

"That Dustin?" Willow looked around the room to see who I was talking to.

"Sorry, yes," I said. "Dustin's going to look around with us."

"The more the merrier," Willow said.

Everyone seemed happy because that meant Oreo would be coming too. They were all big fans of Oreo.

After checking every inch of the gym, we were able to determine that the portal wasn't there, but as soon as we got to the cafeteria, I felt the familiar abrupt temperature change. During lunch, I had assumed that the room was cold because there was so much ghost activity, but now that the ghosts had wandered into other locations in the school, I realized that the temperature was just as chilly as it had been earlier.

"The portal is here." My warm breath plumed into the air.

"I see what you meant by the temperature thing."

Fatima exhaled deeply so that her breath cloud floated in front of her as well. "It's freezing."

"There is a strong energy in here," Dustin said matter-of-factly. "I didn't realize it before because I was too busy trying to avoid plates of food getting thrown at my head, but I can definitely sense it now."

Based on how he looked, I don't think he actually avoided much of anything. His clothes were still peppered with the same food stains from earlier.

"But how will we know exactly where the portal is?" Thalia asked.

I was able to answer that question thanks to the notes from my ancestors!

"We have to keep walking around the room until we find the one spot that is colder than the rest." I looked around and noticed that Oreo had jumped down from Dustin's shoulder and was meowing at something over by the salad bar.

"Do you think the portal could be over there?" I asked Dustin. "Oreo seems really interested in that one section of the cafeteria."

"Must be," Dustin said. "But how are we going to get all the spirits in the building to come here?"

"I have a plan." I pulled out my candles from my back-pack. "Think you can manage to start another food fight, Dustin? It might be our best chance to lure the rest of the ghosts into the cafeteria."

"But I just got the pasta out of my hair," he groaned.

I shot him a dirty look since I could clearly see he defi-nitely still had pasta in his ashy brown hair, which was sticking up in all sorts of directions.

"I'm just kidding," he said. "I'd be happy to help. I'm just going to leave Oreo with Barry so that he doesn't get trampled."

"Good thinking!" I said.

I let Willow, Thalia, and Fatima know what was going on.

"Do you think we can live stream this?" Thalia asked. "I feel like this would be good content for your page."

"I don't see why not." I shrugged.

After a few minutes, we heard Dustin's voice bellow, "FOOD FIGHT!" and a swarm of ghosts exploded into the cafeteria. It looked like Dustin was leading them into battle! As all the ghosts started pelting each other with spectral food, I lit my candles and focused on sending them all (except Dustin, of course) back through the portal. Which was easier said than done with all the mess around me.

I concentrated extra hard, since there were so many spirits to send back and worried that there might be some stragglers hiding out in the school, like Willow's grandpa, who was noticeably absent. But I'd have to think about them later and focus on getting the majority out of here.

The room began to shake more violently than usual, causing some of the cafeteria chairs and part of the salad bar to topple over. A heavy gust of wind followed by a warm stillness filled the air. I opened my eyes to find everyone's hair looking particularly windblown. Dustin's stood straight up, which was somehow worse than how it looked before, and Willow's normally crunchy curls now closely resembled the teased style from her party. Fatima and Thalia were both wearing their hair tightly pulled back. Fatima had hers in her signature braid and Thalia's was in a bun, so they only had a few stray pieces to contend with.

I felt a wave of relief wash over me knowing that most of the spirits were now safely back through the portal. As I put my supplies away, I realized I had used almost all of my candles to send all these ghosts through to the other side. I'd need to find a way to get more soon if I wanted to send any leftover spirits back and still have enough to do my readings.

"Do you think we got all of them?" Barry asked, peeking into the room. He was holding Oreo outstretched from his body since the cat was wriggling intensely, trying to make his way back over to Dustin. It looked like Oreo had gotten his claws into Barry. His security hall monitor sash was now torn to shreds.

"I'm pretty sure we got most of them." I took off my necklace to wipe off some of the ectoplasmic goo that had gotten on it from the food fight and put it in my pocket. "Keep me posted if you see any rogue ghosts floating around, and I'll be sure to send them back."

"I'll keep an eye out," Barry replied.

"That was our highest number of views yet!" Thalia exclaimed. "Your page is more popular than ever, Paloma!"

She pinned back one of her flyaway overly bleached strands back into place. Her dark roots looked like they had been growing back in for a while.

"This is awesome!" Fatima peeked over Thalia's shoulder to get a better look at the viewership statistics. I was

194

concentrating so hard on what I was doing that I forgot they were recording!

My stomach sank and I remembered something else that had taken a back seat during the ghost chaos of the day: Willow's grandpa and what he asked me to do. Suddenly I could barely look at Willow. How could I keep this from her? How could I tell her?

I still had no idea what to do and now the yellow carnations were back to popping up everywhere like a bad case of hiccups that wouldn't go away.

"Can we meet this weekend to go over strategy for your page?" Willow asked excitedly, oblivious to my inner turmoil. "I think we can make this thing really big and reach more than just the kids at our school."

"Oh! And maybe you could do a reading for one of us so we can see how many classmates tune in for a weekend live stream," Thalia suggested.

They were all so eager to help me, and it just made me feel even guiltier. But maybe I didn't have to make a decision right away. Instead, I could just focus on Totally Psychic and building up my profile enough that Abuela would be begging me to join her on the Latin America tour.

"Sure!" I said, pushing my worried feelings as far down as they would go. "That would be perfect."

Abuela was going to be seriously impressed.

15

A Difference of Opinion

When I got home from school, Mom was waiting for me in the living room. By the way her eyes squinted in my direction, I wondered if Aunt Maria decided to rat me out for what happened at Willow's slumber party after all. Mom had that knowing look in her eye that usually meant she caught me doing something that I wasn't supposed to be doing.

"You have some explaining to do, young lady." She had a disapproving scowl on her face. "I just heard from your school. Is it true that you've been having online readings in the middle of class? Here I was thinking you were starting to adjust and make friends, when all this time you've been interrupting the learning process for other students. I should have known better than to trust that you had stopped talking to ghosts."

"But I was doing it during my free periods!" I exclaimed. "It's not like I was skipping class or anything."

I hoped if I didn't make any sudden movements, she wouldn't notice my attempt at escape to my bedroom. I took a small step toward the hall. At least she didn't know about the spirit portal problem.

"Your principal called to let me know that the other students were all on their phones during class to watch your reading last week." Mom's dark brown eyes narrowed. She didn't seem to care about any excuses. "Paloma, I thought we discussed this. You aren't here to be playing medium. Ghosts are the same thing as strangers. I don't want you talking to them."

"Okay, so should I do the readings after school then?" I threw my backpack onto the couch not realizing that Beryl was sitting there.

"Sorry," I mouthed to Beryl who rubbed the side of her body where it had landed.

"So that's why you stayed late today, is it? To answer your question, no, you should not be doing these readings at all." Mom paced around the room, anger in each step. "You know, I have the perfect solution for keeping you out of trouble."

I did not like the sound of that. I moved a few more inches toward my bedroom.

"You'll be spending your time after school at church choir practice. And as for your weekends, you'll be helping with the flower truck," Mom said, still patrolling the room. "This way, you won't have any spare time for trouble or readings or anything else. There's a farmer's market this weekend. You'll be on bouquet-wrapping duty. You hear me?"

You would not think such an angry person worked with flowers all day. Those calming fragrances had no effect on her.

"But, Mom, I'm supposed to hang out with my new friends this weekend! I promised Willow, Fatima, and Thalia. I can't just bail on them now."

Part of me worried that they wouldn't want to be my friends anymore if I wasn't around to do readings. But there was no way I could help Mom out *and* hang out with them…or could I?

"You'll just have to tell your friends you'll see them some

other time." Mom rubbed her temples like she usually did when she was trying to collect her anger. "I am glad you are making friends, Paloma. But you have to understand there are consequences for your actions. Maybe next quarter once I start seeing some good grades from you and I don't get any more calls from the principal's office, you can have a social life again. And why aren't you wearing the necklace Aunt Rosa gave you?"

I touched my neck and realized I must have forgotten to put it back on.

Why did she even care about the necklace anyway? Can't Mom just be mad at one thing at a time?

"Ugh!" I stomped my way to my room and plopped face-first on the bed.

I screamed into my pillow before reaching to grab the amethyst necklace from my pocket and hooked it around my neck—at least that was one problem fixed.

"What's the matter?" Beryl peeked her head through my door. "Is it okay if I come in?"

I waved her inside.

Before I could say anything, Magdalena barged into my room. She was holding up her phone in front of her face, probably playing some virtual reality game.

"What are you doing in here?" I asked.

I was surprised Magdalena hadn't tried worming her way in here sooner. And what was she doing holding a hatbox under her arm? Sometimes with Magdalena it was best not to ask too many questions.

"Oh!" She immediately put her phone down by her side. "Sorry, I didn't realize you were in here."

"If you didn't realize I was in here then why are you in here?" She was so hard to figure out.

"I was uh…" She paused. "Looking for your diary."

That tracked.

"Can you go?" My voice went up an octave on the last vowel.

Magdalena darted out of the room.

"You see what I have to put up with?" My attention was back to Beryl who sat on top of a laundry basket in the corner of my room. "And to answer your question, I have to help out with Mom's flower truck this weekend, but I promised my new friends I'd meet with them to talk about our social media strategy for @TotallyPsychic. I don't want to get in any more trouble with Mom, but I don't want them to kick me out of the group either."

"You can do both," Harrison shouted from the window box.

Classic Harrison, always eavesdropping.

"That sounds great and all," I said as I opened the window so that I could hear him better. "The only problem is, Mom pretty much has eyes in the back of her head. She always knows when I'm doing something even when I'm not doing something. It's freaky."

"Shouldn't be an issue," Harrison said. "Invite your friends to the farmer's market and find a moment to slip away from helping your mom to meet them."

"Normally I wouldn't encourage this kind of behavior, but Harrison must be getting to me," Beryl said. "Making friends is important, but so is listening to your mother. Oh, what the hay, give the old kook's advice a shot."

"You'd be back before she even realizes what happened," Harrison added.

"Guess that could work if I timed things right." As much as I wanted to trust the plan of two ghosts, I decided to call Jasmin and Keisha to get a second opinion. The more validation the better!

Once Harrison and Beryl disappeared from sight, I video

chatted with my best friends from Miami. They'd know what to do.

"I need some advice," I said as soon as their images popped up on my phone.

"Um, hello to you too? This is actually perfect timing," Keisha said, "because we were actually going to call you tonight anyway to get *your* opinion on something."

An echo boomed.

"Are you both in the same room?" Keisha's bedroom was in the background, her hot pink wall with glitter stencil hearts a dead giveaway. It looked exactly the same since we were in kindergarten. Only now there were more twinkly lights and posters of K-pop stars these days.

"Yeah!" Jasmin said. Her hair matched the color of Keisha's room. "Sorry, I'll hang up!"

Jasmin ended the call and moved closer to Keisha so that they were both in frame on the screen.

"So, what's up?" Jasmin asked.

"I am basically grounded for the rest of my life because Mom somehow found out about the readings I had been doing." I winced. "And now I can't even see my friends this weekend. It could seriously mess up my new friendship with Willow, Thalia, and Fatima, right? Will they even want to still hang out with me if I can't see them after school for months? Like, they'll probably just forget that I exist."

My mouth felt instantly drier, making it harder to talk.

"Do you think you could cool it with the readings for a little while?" Jasmin asked. "Maybe lie low for a bit?"

"I don't really have time to lie low," I said. "I'm still trying to impress my grandma so she'll take me on tour with her in a little over a month. And these readings are the only way I can prove to her that I'm ready!"

I pulled up the countdown app on my phone. I only had seven more weeks before she left.

"Hold up a second. Since when are you going on tour with your grandma?" Keisha raised her eyebrows. "Doesn't she normally go on those solo?"

"I mean, I'm not. At least not yet." I bit my lip. "She only said no the first time I asked because I wasn't ready, but now I actually am! I'm hoping that after she sees what I've been up to, she'll change her mind and reconsider taking me."

"Why don't you talk to her about it?" Jasmin asked. "You can't expect her to be a mind reader."

"Besides, there's always next year's tour. And I'm sure your friends will be understanding that you have to see them some other time." Keisha shrugged. "I mean, I know they're way less cool than us…and you still love us more, but they'll get it."

"Exactly. The truth will set you free! Or something like that," Jasmin said. "Honestly, I wouldn't mess with your mom. It's not worth it. That woman has eyes in the back of her head, I swear."

Okay so it wasn't just me who thought that!

"The ghosts in my house think that I could probably get away with sneaking off to meet with them while I'm helping Mom. I know I can pull it off." I grabbed Oscar and put him on my lap for emotional support. I started tapping on one of his plastic eyes. So much for validation.

"Oooh bad idea. Like big-time," Keisha said. "I agree with Jasmin on this one. If you get caught, your mom's never going to let you have a social life again. I want to be able to see you sometime before you're eighty. I say don't do it."

"Seriously," Jasmin said, regaining control of the camera. "Like that time she knew about that R-rated movie we snuck into and she tipped off all of our parents and they all showed up at the theatre to pick us up? I didn't see either of you for a month."

Yeah, that was the worst. It ruined our entire summer break last year since we all ended up being grounded.

"I do like to think my sneak skills have improved since then though." I nervously chewed on one of my cuticles. "I feel like the ghosts might be right on this one. This situation is totally manageable. Mom will be too distracted with customers to even notice that I'm gone."

"Well, it was nice knowing you," Keisha said. "Now, can you help us with something?"

"Sure, anything," I said.

"Jasmin and I are working on a group project for school, but Eloise keeps ruining it." Keisha looked behind her, I assumed to double-check that Eloise was still elsewhere. "We don't know how to get her to stop."

Why would they replace me with someone who kept ruining their stuff? Eloise sounded pretty terrible. But if they knew I was jealous, I would never hear the end of it.

"Have you tried working on your project when she isn't around?" I hugged Oscar a little tighter.

"Only issue with that is…she's always around." Jasmin shrugged.

Yikes, the clingy type. At least I didn't have to worry about them liking their new friend more than me.

CRASH!

"Shoot," Keisha said. "Eloise again. We've got to go."

The call ended.

Guess good friends were hard to come by in Florida these days. Sounded like Eloise was more of a chaos monster than Magdalena.

My fingers itched as I debated what to do. Should I listen to the ghosts or my friends? Ghosts were much older and wiser so they were probably right. It was also the option that I wanted to do, so I decided to go for it. I texted my new group chat and told them that we were all set to meet up at the farmer's market on Saturday. I'd be able to do a reading for them as soon as I could get away from the flower truck.

Nothing could go wrong!

16

FARMER'S MARKET

Most of Saturday morning was spent packing up Mom's truck with buckets of flowers. Mom had them grouped by color with the names and descriptions written on tiny chalkboard signs. The vehicle may have been super old, like straight out of the 1960s old, but with the new mint green paint job and the way Mom had all the flowers arranged in the back, it was looking extra cute. The new logo for Flor's Flowers was stenciled on the driver's side door with its big white swirly font popping out against the mint green exterior.

As cool as it was, I still missed her store in Miami. That was the place where I first fell in love with flowers. My favorite memories were at the shop. The aroma of hundreds of varieties of flowers lingering in the warm Miami air. It was like being embraced by a fragrant hug. The smell of all the flowers in the truck brought me back to that place.

I was still pretty mad at Mom, but flowers always made things a little easier between us somehow. I blamed the calming effects of lavender. I was always in a better mood when I was around her plants.

"I really do appreciate you helping me with the farmer's market today." Mom lifted another box into the truck. "I know I've been hard on you lately, but it's only because I believe in your potential."

Abuela believed in my potential too. If Mom really meant that, she would stop getting so mad at me all the time. Her ability to run between hot and cold emotions was unbelievable. If the other kids at school wanted to watch my readings during class time, that was their problem. I wasn't the one being irresponsible here.

I climbed over a box of parchment paper intended for wrapping flowers. There wasn't much room in the truck for passengers so I had to squeeze next to Magdalena on the back bench while trying not to crush the box of ranunculus bouquets that sat in between us. Apparently she was too young to stay home by herself, so Mom said she had to come.

Once we got to the farmer's market, Mom parked between a booth selling vegan dog treats and a blacksmith. I helped her pull down the striped awning on the side of the truck and hang up the twinkle lights which made our stall look extra cozy and welcoming.

The farmer's market was a lot more crowded than I had expected, so Mom was sure to be distracted by customers. All was going according to plan.

But even before we were fully set up, dozens of people lined up for bouquets. There was even a frustrated ghost trying to get her attention. I was really busy helping Mom, and although she was smiling a lot while talking to each customer, I could see the stress behind her eyes. Sneaking away was going to be harder than I thought. My stomach squeezed. To make things worse, my phone was exploding with messages from Willow asking where I was.

I sent a quick text back while Mom was arranging a bouquet for the next person in line. My message to Willow just said, "green truck." It was all I could manage to type before I had to help with the next customer. It was getting busier by the second!

I also hadn't counted on Magdalena tagging along. Now I had another family member to tiptoe past. To make matters worse, Magdalena was also apparently too young to actually do any work at the flower stand even though I had been helping Mom out at the store at her age. So that meant I was going to have a nine-year-old bossing me around all day, watching my every move with her beady little eyes. Knowing what Magdalena was like, she would be waiting for me to make the slightest mistake so that she could run to Mom, cementing her role as the favorite.

My only option was to let her in on my plan and pray to the chaos gods that she wouldn't tattle. We'd have to make a deal…and I hated making deals with her.

"Magdalena." I turned to my sister. "I need you to do me the favor of all favors."

Clearly, I was desperate.

"That depends," she said, sniffing a bright red dahlia. "What's the favor?"

"Can you please cover me for ten minutes while I take care of something?" I wasn't going to tell her what I was actually doing—I was smarter than that.

Her hazel eyes pierced deep inside my soul.

"I'm going to tell Mom." Magdalena dropped the flower

she had been holding onto the ground and pivoted toward Mom, who was talking to a customer about a bouquet of peonies.

Come on!

"Magdalena, please," I said. "I never ask you for anything. What about the bonds of sisterhood Aunt Rosa was talking about before we moved here? We're supposed to have each other's backs." I pointed to the amethyst bracelet on her wrist.

She looked down at the bracelet, taking it off for a second to examine the beads of amethyst as if they would tell her what she needed to do.

"Alright, fine." She slipped the bracelet back on her wrist.

I couldn't believe that actually worked!

"Thank you for not being the worst this one time." I gave her a giant hug, which she immediately pulled away from.

"I'm going to run over to one of the other stands to grab a snack, I'll be right back!" I shouted to Mom over the sound of her Celia Cruz streaming station that she always liked to listen to while she worked. It also helped my chances of escape that she was still distracted talking to customers.

"Okay!" Mom replied. "But make sure it's quick."

Even if Mom was against me running off, she was never going to say it in front of a customer. Mom hated making a scene at work.

So far, the plan was off to a great start.

I spotted Willow and the others over by a stand called Percy's Pickles. The sign advertised one hundred flavors of pickles, which was interesting because I didn't realize pickles came in other flavors besides "pickle." It even had a large group of ghosts waiting in line. And maybe I was imagining things, but the ghost working at the stand really looked suspiciously like Willow's grandfather. Could he be following me? I shook off my paranoia and slid onto the bench beside Thalia, who was taste testing a pickle variety pack that included mint and bubble gum flavors. Yuck.

"Hey!" I waved. "Sorry to keep you waiting. I needed to find a good moment to sneak away!"

"No worries," Fatima said as she applied a heap of SPF 50 to her face. "If now isn't a good time, we can do this another day."

She handed the bottle of sunscreen to Thalia, who looked like she needed it. I could see the sunburn beginning to emerge on her lightly tanned skin.

"Now is fine!" I said. I realized that Jasmin and Keisha were right about my new friends being understanding. I really should start listening to them more.

I reached my hand out to borrow some of her sunscreen, making sure to take off my necklace from Aunt Rosa first so that it wouldn't get gross. Even though the temperature was similar to what it was back in Miami, there was something about the heat that made it feel like my mouth was drying out every time I took a breath. I put my amethyst pendant back around my neck.

"We don't want to get you in trouble or anything if you have to help your mom at the flower stand. We can just talk about our social media strategy during lunch next week," Willow said, taking a sip of her oversized frozen coffee. Her face was shaded by the large hat she was wearing. "It's no biggie. Honestly, this has been exactly what I needed today. My parents have been fighting a lot lately, so it was kind of nice to have the excuse to get out of the house."

I pressed my lips together tightly as I tried to hide any expression that I knew what she was talking about. I busied myself by fiddling with my phone, opening Instagram and propping my phone up against Thalia's giant coffee to take a group selfie with my friends.

"Yeah, it's totally fine to just hang out here! Just make sure you stay clear of the ice cream stand," Fatima warned. She had a cup full of melted ice cream in front of her. "The vendor is apparently testing out some flavors for next month's garlic festival. It's disgusting."

"Noted." I looked over at the melted puddle filled with raw garlic chunks.

Wow, they were being way more understanding than I expected… If I left now, I could probably head back to Mom's flower truck before she started to get suspicious as to why I've been gone for so long.

But before I could say goodbye to my friends, I heard the dreaded sound of Mom's voice booming behind me.

"Ay, dios mío. You have got to be kidding me!" she shouted.

My head whipped around so fast I was pretty sure I was going to be sick. The vein in Mom's neck looked like it was going to escape from her body.

Uh-oh. My stomach dropped. Why had I trusted Magdalena?

Mom grabbed my phone off the table and then turned to my friends and recomposed herself.

"Hi, I'm Paloma's mom." She clenched her teeth in a forced smile. "Paloma needs to come back with me to the flower stand. It's a busy afternoon. I'm sure you understand."

There was a resounding look of shock on all of their faces as Willow took off her sunglasses and slowly nodded. They could definitely tell I was in serious trouble.

I closed my eyes tight, hoping I could be invisible. I knew the second I was alone with Mom, I was going to hear her go off on me for disobeying her order to stop doing my readings. And I wasn't even going to do one this time! But I guess she did also tell me that I couldn't hang out with my friends, so there was no talking my way out of this one.

When we got back to the flower truck, Magdalena's eyes went wide. She looked more surprised than I was. If this was her plan all along, she really shouldn't be this shocked. I bet she knew I was on to her for being a traitor. This would be the last time I'd trust Magdalena, that was for sure.

"I can't believe you told!" I shouted at my sister. "That's what I get for trusting the bonds of sisterhood."

"I didn't this time!" She drew an X against her chest with her index finger. "Cross my heart, I swear."

Yeah right. If she was trying to play both sides, I wasn't falling for it.

"You mean to tell me you were in on it too?" Mom turned her scolding attention to Magdalena. "You need to stop letting your sister be such a bad influence on you."

Huh, maybe Magdalena was telling the truth after all. The bonds of sisterhood were back on. As much as I enjoyed the idea of Magdalena falling out of Mom's-pet status, it wasn't fair for her to get in trouble for something I did.

"To be fair, I didn't tell her what I was actually going to be doing," I said. "She just thought I was hungry and needed to grab a snack over at the pickle stand."

"Consider both of your social lives canceled for the next month," Mom said.

Jasmin and Keisha were right. That's the last time I listen to the ghosts.

17

Busted

It was kind of hard to be grounded to a bedroom when the room didn't even have any locks, but I knew better than to leave the safety of my room. Mom was still majorly peeved at what happened at the farmer's market. It apparently wasn't just the fact that she thought I was doing the reading that made her so upset, it was that I tried to trick her to see my friends, who she already told me I couldn't hang out with.

Anyway, I was officially banned from doing any more readings and now Mom would be paying closer attention to my every move, so I was going to need to be a lot more careful about doing my live readings, if I was even going to continue to do them at all. Just in case, I decided to make my page officially private and combed through my follower list to make sure everyone looked teenagery and not like a mom-spy account. But I had to face the reality of the situation, that my days of being an online medium were over. There were going to be no more readings from me anytime soon. My followers were going to be so disappointed! Though no one was going to be more disappointed than myself.

During my first period class on Monday, I was surprised to find Stephen Sato standing over by my desk. What did he want to bother me about? At least he didn't have flowers swirling around him anymore.

"Hey, I just want to say I'm sorry for what happened at the farmer's market this weekend," he said. "I saw what happened at your mom's truck. My parents own the vegan dog-treat business that your family was parked next to so I sort of heard the whole thing."

"Why do you care about that anyway?" I felt embarrassed that he saw me get in trouble.

"I know I gave you a hard time on your first day, but your powers are actually pretty cool and you've been helping a lot of the other students around here, including me. Minus the whole squish butt thing, it was really nice to hear from my aunt," Stephen said. "So basically what I'm trying to say is, I don't think you should stop doing what you're doing."

"Thanks, Stephen…that's surprisingly nice to hear." I had been feeling guilty for embarrassing him with the squish butt hashtag I created. "And I'm sorry for repeating your aunt's nickname for the whole school to hear. I kind of got carried away with that one."

"All good," he said. "I definitely should've been nicer to you when you first moved here, so we're even."

Stephen was right. I couldn't give up on Totally Psychic just because Mom wanted me to. I was actually starting to make some real friends and I was getting a chance to help people, just like Abuela. If I could get enough of a following, Abuela would realize how valuable I'd be on tour with her. But I was starting to run out of time. There were only a few weeks left until her tour. I needed to step up my game, even if I was in the danger zone for more punishments. I had back-to-back readings booked for lunch today that I had no intention of canceling.

The first: Ines Rodriguez from language arts class with Miss Gustavo. Ines was one of the first people to message me about a reading on Instagram. I wasn't going to get caught a second time, so I messaged Ines to meet me in the custodial closet so we'd have extra privacy. This meant there would be no production crew due to space issues. I texted the group to let them know that I would be doing this one solo. The closet was tiny, but it was still big enough to fit Ines and me for a reading. And since there weren't any windows, I chose not to risk using candles for fire safety reasons. Plus, there was the slight issue that my supply was seriously low after the fiasco that followed Willow's sleepover party.

I was still a little nervous after what happened with the Ouija board. More nervous than I thought I'd be. I'd done dozens of these readings, but for whatever reason my stomach felt like it was doing more flips than an Olympic gymnast.

"Is this the right place?" Ines asked as she cracked the door open and squeezed herself inside.

The closet was much more crowded with two people than I expected. I was squished next to all of the cleaning supplies and paint cans to make room for Ines to sit next to me. There was barely going to be enough room for a ghost.

Ines sat down on the other overturned bucket I'd placed on the floor. Not my usual ambiance, but it would have to do. I propped my phone up against a bottle of ammonia to fit us both in the frame. We were officially live streaming, though I wasn't sure how much my viewers could actually see since the lighting was so bad.

I took a deep breath and began to concentrate as I entered into a brief meditative state like Abuela had taught me. A mop and broom hit the floor as the portal to the spirit world opened. I covered my head in case anything else decided to fall from one of the many shelves that were filled with cleaning supplies and containers.

Two spirits crossed over the threshold at the same time, which was something I'd never seen before. A middle-aged bald man with narrow eyes and a crooked smile shoved an elderly woman back through to the other side. As she vanished from sight through the invisible portal, he glided over to the top of the utility shelves, swinging his legs gleefully. He looked pleased with himself for successfully attacking an old lady. Not cool.

I went on with the reading as usual as if nothing strange had happened, relaying what I had seen for Ines and the Instagram live audience.

"A spirit has successfully crossed over from the other side." I looked up at the man, who was still swinging his legs. "He's an older bald gentleman with a large mustache. Does this sound like anyone you know?"

"Not really..." Ines bit her cheek. She looked upward trying to search her memory for someone fitting the description, but I could tell she was drawing a blank. She twisted her mouth to the other side and shrugged. "No, nothing is coming to mind."

Hmm, I was going to have to be a little more direct with this spirit to get some answers.

"Spirit, it seems Ines doesn't know you from my description. Do you mind telling us who you are and what your relationship is to Ines?" I asked. "And who was the older woman that you were crossing over with?"

"That old broad?" he floated down to one of the lower shelves so that he was now at eye level with me and Ines. His forehead was creased with hard set lines. "I'm a much better time than old Abuela Carmen there. Tell Ines it's her

223

favorite primo, Gino, here to see her." He spread his arms out wide, his left hand sticking through a box of bleach.

"Do you have a cousin named Gino?" I asked. "He was so excited to see you that he cut the line in front of your grandmother and knocked her back into the spirit world."

"Are you trying to tell me Cousin Gino who I've barely even met in my entire life ruined my chances of talking to my abuela?" Ines's face was turning red. "My grandma was my best friend! I lived with her for most of my child-hood! Tell him I want to talk to her. You can bring her back, can't you? He's not even a close relative. I barely even knew him!"

I could relate to her being so close with her grandma. I felt so bad Ines's reading had taken such a turn.

"Aw come on, don't be so sore about it," Gino said, frowning. "I'm the one who was always the life of the party."

He floated in circles around the room in an attempt to prove how fun he was. I don't think he realized she couldn't see him.

"I want a redo!" Ines demanded, close to tears.

"I'm so sorry," I said. Did this happen because I didn't use the candles? I closed my eyes and began to concentrate extra hard to send him back, but nothing happened. I grabbed the candle out of my bag and lit it briefly to help get Gino back to where he came from. This time it worked. The room shook and an entire shelf of cleaning supplies began to fall over as the portal opened.

"No, come on, please," Gino said. "Don't send me back. I don't want to go back down there."

Down there?

Oh, that wasn't good. If he was referring to what I think he was, then he was a bad spirit!

Not good. Not good. Seriously, not good.

I closed my eyes and concentrated even harder on sending him back before he could do any more damage. I felt sweat pouring down my forehead until eventually, Cousin Gino was gone.

I should have learned my lesson after what happened at Willow's party.

"I'm so sorry, Ines," I said again. "That shouldn't have happened."

"It's not your fault." She got up. "Cousin Gino shouldn't have done that. Do you mind if we try again some other time?"

"I'd be happy to." I tried to smile my way through this because it was more my fault than I wanted her to know. I really needed to get a hold of some more candles since I was down to my last candle nub. Now that I knew what could happen if I didn't properly set up for a reading, I could make sure something like this never happened again.

I waved at Ines as she moved past the maze of fallen buckets on her way out of the room and pressed myself against the wall the moment that she was gone. My heart felt like it was about to fly out of my chest from beating so fast. I was going to have to do the next reading from the greenhouse like normal with my last remaining candle. I didn't want to mess things up again. I texted the group chat to see if Willow, Thalia, and Fatima would be around to help. They were already set up with the equipment in the greenhouse before I even got there.

I was glad that most of the spirits that had escaped through the spirit portal were now gone, but I did keep running into a few in the halls that I knew I still needed to get rid of. It just wasn't a big enough issue for me to focus on now. Sending the remaining ghosts back would have to wait. The only annoying thing was that Willow's grand-father liked to turn up wherever Willow was, so he was standing with us in the greenhouse repeating the words *tell her* over and over again. I did my best to ignore him, hoping that he would just go away on his own. Maybe I'd be able to send him back through the spirit portal after my reading with Jeremy! But unfortunately, he disappeared before I even got started. Which I guess was good for the reading, but not good for the fact that I wanted him out of my hair once and for all.

Thankfully, Jeremy Barnes's reading went much smoother. Jeremy's old neighbor, Big John, and a dozen chickens came through for him almost immediately.

Willow, Thalia, and Fatima all seemed to be equally de-lighted over the concept of ghost chickens. Some of the chickens ran in circles around Big John while the others enjoyed their new flying abilities that they didn't have in life. These birds were pretty entertaining to watch.

Jeremy revealed that Big John used to babysit him while his parents were at work and that he spent a lot of time helping John tend to an illegal chicken coop that he had in his backyard. Even though it was a little hard to make out what Big John was saying over the sound of a dozen squawking chickens, it was sweet that the chickens were still connected to him in the afterlife. Overall, it was a very good reading. Jeremy couldn't have been happier. This definitely made up for the Ines custodial closet catastrophe. Phew! And I even had enough candle left for one more reading.

Another thing I was grateful for today besides not having to deal with any more unwanted ghosts was the fact that I wouldn't have to face Mom back at the house later. She was still pretty mad about the farmer's market disaster. But thankfully Mom and Dad had an anniversary date night, so at least I didn't have to deal with more of her punishments. The downside: I'd have to spend the entire evening with Magdalena by myself. So maybe that was the punishment.

By the time I got home, tropical storm Magdalena had already wreaked her havoc on the house, turning it into a disaster zone. Mom was not going to be happy. Pillows were thrown everywhere, pictures on the wall were crooked, and a trail of blankets lined the hall. Even one of the curtains had been pulled down. It was a complete and total mess. How did she accomplish so much destruction in the short amount of time she was home before me?

"You owe me big time. You owe me big time," Magdalena sang as she ran circles around me like she was a human airplane. It reminded me of Big John's chickens.

"What are you even talking about?" I picked the pillows off the floor and put them back onto the couch.

"You did another live reading today even after Mom told you to stop." She wiggled her eyebrows at me.

Every part of me wanted to scream, but I decided to play it cool in case she was bluffing.

"How do you know that?" I cleared my throat. "I mean, I don't know what you're talking about."

So much for playing it cool.

"I saw it! I saw it! Now you have to do whatever I tell you to for a week orrrrrrrrr I'm telling Mom." She jumped onto the couch. "*And* you have to let me do whatever I want tonight."

"Fine! Whatever!" I stormed off into the kitchen to grab myself a snack. But when I opened the cabinet, it wasn't a box of cereal staring back at me, it was Beryl. "How did

229

you get in there? Or, I guess I should say, why are you in there?"

"Shhh," Beryl replied, pressing a finger to her lips. "I wasn't going to say anything at first because I always feel that siblings should sort things out themselves, but I think there's something you need to know."

I reminded myself that I wasn't going to listen to her or Harrison anymore since they were partially why I was in trouble in the first place.

"Beryl, you aren't making any sense right now." I tried reaching past her for the box of rice crisps.

"You may want to pull out your phone and look up something called Ghost-Tok," she said with a sigh.

I never really used TikTok that much, but I opened the app to see what Beryl was talking about. After getting sucked into the vortex of distraction and watching five different videos on how to make your own soap, I found an account called Ghost-Tok, and my mouth dropped open.

I couldn't believe it.

There was footage of Beryl and Harrison wandering around the house. *Our* house.

"This can't be possible," I said. "People can't just videotape ghosts. Can they?" I clicked through more videos, trying to figure out some way that this could be fake. Most of them were of Beryl doing things like opening cabinets and floating through walls. There were a couple more of the skateboarding ghosts on our block that I had waved hello to on our first day here. There was even a ghost trying to buy produce from stands at the farmer's market. I zoomed closer and saw that it was Willow's grandfather, which confirmed my suspicion that he was following me.

These were all ghosts that I'd seen in real life, so it couldn't be fake. My heart raced. Whoever was videotaping them had to be someone in the family. These were our ghosts on here. This was real. Which meant—

The thought crossed my mind of who was behind this. But it couldn't be…could it? Every single part of me hoped that I was wrong.

I grabbed my notebook and closed my eyes, trying to do a self-prediction for some reassurance that this was all some sort of big mistake. But nothing happened. I was staring at a blank page. Where were my powers when I needed them?

I ran out of the room and charged right up to my sister. "Magdalena, you have some explaining to do."

Her eyes bulged and her cheeks pinkened. She dropped her phone. "Busted."

18

Ghost-Tok

This could not be happening. No one in our family has ever gotten their powers before their twelfth birthday. Magdalena was way too young! That must mean that she was seriously powerful…

I did not like the sound of that.

The world went out of focus. It felt as if I were surrounded by the chaos hum of a thousand bees.

My dreams of being the next Gloria Jimenez, medium to the stars, came crashing down the second I looked at that video of Beryl and Harrison in our house. Videotaping ghosts was pretty awesome, no matter how much I hated to admit it. Better than my live readings anyway. At least with these, her viewers could actually *see* what was happening! No wonder she had such a huge following! Way more than my account. I couldn't compete with that.

She couldn't just let me have this one thing to myself?

Magdalena's eyes darted toward her bedroom door, and I knew she was going to make a break for it. Before she could, I angled myself like a human obstacle to block her from getting past me.

Her back foot pivoted slightly and her tiny frame pushed against me with all her might. I wouldn't be able to hold her back for much longer. Her powerfulness was apparently not limited to her ability to communicate with ghosts.

I had to think of a different strategy, and quick. *Come on brain!* But only one option came to mind, and it was a tall order: I was going to have to reason with her. It was my only hope.

In other words, a nearly impossible task.

"Stop!" I tried to get her to stand still, but she pulled away and took a few steps backward. Before I could say anything more, she leaped past me like I was a human track hurdle.

"I'm not going to tell Mom!" I shouted in a last-ditch effort to get her to stay. She stopped in her tracks just inches from the door and turned to face me in what seemed like slow motion. I couldn't believe that actually worked.

"You're not?" Magdalena slipped her phone back into her pocket. Her entire face twisted up in confusion.

"No," I sighed. I walked closer to where she was standing. My hands were up in the air to show her that I came in peace. I was completely wasting my chance to get back at her for all the years of being blamed for her pranks, but she was still my little sister and I knew that figuring out new powers alone was already hard enough. I looked down at my necklace and reminded myself of the bonds that Aunt Rosa said we shared. We both needed each other.

"Oh." She eyed me skeptically, her face still scrunched. "Well, why not?"

"Because we need each other." If Magdalena had powers, as annoying as that was, we were going to have to stick together in this house.

She sat down on one of her pillow towers from her earlier episode of tornado-ing through the living room. "Do you actually mean it?" Her eyes peeked out from the top of a pillow.

"I swear." I extended my pinky, and she hesitantly hooked hers through it. "So, when did you realize you could see ghosts anyway?"

I took a seat on our pastel-colored couch and patted the cushion next to me, inviting Magdalena to sit down.

"It started around when we first got here." Magdalena crawled out of her pillow cocoon and onto the couch. "It took a few days until I started to see a man and a woman ghost show up when I opened the camera on my phone. They weren't the skateboarding ones you were talking about on our first day here that got Mom super upset. But that's why I've been running around the house so much. I was trying to catch the ghosts on my phone's camera but they kept hiding or trying to get away from me."

"Oh, that explains…so much. I just thought you were super hyper. Have you talked to them at all?" I asked.

At least now I knew why she destroyed half the house. She was just trying to get Beryl and Harrison on video.

"No," Magdalena buried her face in her lap. "I'm not able to talk to them like you can. I can only see them on my camera." She scrolled through her photos and handed me her phone to show me what she meant. "This is my first ghost pic."

I looked at the photo of Beryl in her translucent form standing behind Magdalena in her mirror. If you didn't look carefully, you could almost mistake the ghost for being a living person. After zooming in though, I could see the hints of Magdalena's bedroom through Beryl's scrubs.

"This is really cool stuff." I examined the picture closely. "I've never seen anything like this."

"I was taking a mirror pic of one of my outfits," Magdalena continued, "and this woman was standing behind me in the photo. It kind of freaked me out at first until I talked to Abuela about it, since I obviously couldn't talk to Mom because she hates this stuff. Abuela told me I was getting my powers early and that this was just a glimpse of what I'll be able to do once I turn twelve. She thinks the stress of the move triggered it."

Wait, Abuela knew about this and didn't tell me? As much as I realized this wasn't her secret to tell, I couldn't help but feel super annoyed she didn't bother saying anything about it.

Magdalena didn't notice my mood shift and carried on, saying, "It's why I go around the house filming all the time. I want to see who turns up. Except it's only ever that guy and woman ghost. I think my followers are getting tired of them."

"Harrison and I are very entertaining, thank you!" I could hear Beryl shout through the wall. She was eavesdropping.

No wonder Beryl needed me to interfere! She couldn't actually talk to Magdalena to tell her to stop.

"It's okay if she films us," Beryl said after manifesting back into the room. "I just don't want to be surprised by it. Could there be some way for her to announce her intentions?"

I filled Magdalena in on who the ghosts she'd been filming were and relayed Beryl's message. At least that was one thing I could do that she couldn't!

"They don't mind you filming, as long as you announce when you are going to use your camera," I said. "Ghosts like their privacy more than you'd think, so it's always good to ask permission."

"Oh no, I didn't realize I was upsetting them." Magdalena frowned and slinked deeper into the couch. "I feel super bad."

"Now you know for next time!" I tried my best to sound reassuring. "Boundaries are important, even in the afterlife."

I put my hand on her shoulder the same way Abuela would whenever I made a mistake.

"That's true!" She brightened. "I'm glad there's a way I can keep filming without upsetting the ghosts! Thanks, Paloma!"

Wow, a thank-you from Magdalena? I couldn't believe my ears. The Valley must be freezing over.

"Just curious though, how did you manage to keep it a secret from Mom this whole time? There's no way she wouldn't be suspicious of you filming the ghosts in our house," I said.

I knew Magdalena was sneaky, but Mom's ability to pick up on things was uncanny.

"I'm pretty sure Mom thinks I'm doing weird internet things and talking to my friends on my phone." Magdalena shrugged. "Abuela says spirit photographers are pretty rare, so there wouldn't be much of a reason for Mom to suspect anything. Plus, no one in our family has ever gotten their powers this early, so there's no reason for her to think that I can take pictures of ghosts."

She didn't seem to be too worried about it.

"I just don't want you getting in the same amount of trouble as me for having a ghostly social media presence," I said. "Just make sure you are being careful."

"So you're really not going to tell on me?" Magdalena asked, clutching the pillow to her chest. "Like, for real?"

"No," I sighed. "I think it's better if she doesn't know. There is one thing you can help me with though."

"What?" Magdalena asked.

"Tell me how you got so many followers!" I tossed one of the couch pillows teasingly over to her.

Magdalena was practically at social media famous numbers. What was she doing that I wasn't?

"I don't know," Magdalena confessed. "I've just been doing it for fun as a way to experiment with my powers. I don't think too much about the follower count."

Was fun really the secret to success? Maybe I had been putting too much pressure on myself with these readings. Maybe I just needed to stop thinking about the tour with Abuela and do these readings for me. I deleted the countdown app that was tracking the days that I had left until Abuela's tour on my phone.

Magdalena and I spent the next few hours binge-watching *Everybody's Cousin*. There was a marathon on tonight leading up to a brand-new reunion episode that I had been eagerly awaiting. There were so many plot points I had forgotten about since the last time I watched. Like the episode where they were all stranded on a cruise ship and thought they were being surrounded by sea monsters, but in the end it turned out they were all hallucinating from food poisoning. Classic.

"I never realized Abuela's friend was such a good actress." Magdalena's eyes were glued to the screen.

When our parents got home later that night, they were surprised to find Magdalena and me getting along. They stood silently in the doorway for a solid ten seconds staring at us like we were aliens that had come down from outer space and were posing as their children.

"I half expected this place to be a wreck when we got home," Mom said, finally breaking the silence. Her eye contact was unwavering, like she was waiting for one of us to confess something. "I'm really impressed with you girls."

She examined the living room, running her hand against the lamp shade, pretending to inspect it. Not sure what kind of damage she was looking for, but she wasn't going to find anything here. All of her pillows were back on the couch with me and Magdalena cramped amongst them.

"See, I told you we had nothing to worry about," Dad said as he walked over to where I was sitting. "What are you girls watching?"

"The new live taping of the reunion episode of *Everybody's Cousin*. It's about to come on." I gestured to the television with the remote.

"Is that tonight?" Mom suddenly had an excited bolt of energy in her voice. "Scooch over, I'm watching too."

I squeezed up against Magdalena and the rest of the pillows as Mom took a seat.

"I'll make the popcorn." Dad was already heading toward the kitchen, a giant grin plastered across his face.

He liked it when we got along. It was a rare sighting.

"I wasn't sure if this live taping was still going to come out after what happened with Suzanne La Luca." Mom's eyes were fixated on the screen.

"What do you mean?" I immediately thought back to

the reading with Abuela where Suzanne's aunt warned about an accident. "What happened to Suzanne?"

"You haven't heard?" Mom turned to look at me. "It's been all over the news. Suzanne got in a bad windsurfing accident while they were rehearsing for the episode in Colombia. She was in the hospital for days!"

This must have been what Suzanne's aunt was alluding to during the reading back in Miami. I knew Abuela should have warned her!

"Is she okay?" I couldn't believe I was only just hearing about this now.

"She had amnesia for a little while, which is why they kept her in the hospital for so long. But other than a broken leg, she's okay," Mom said. "I'm sure the writers came up with a creative way to work it into the script."

"Palomaaaa," Magdalena whined, "you made us miss the opening credits."

"Okay, you never even heard of this show until we started watching an hour ago." So much for getting along. I nudged my shoulder into hers teasingly.

"What'd I miss?" Dad salsa danced back in the room with a bowl of popcorn. Extra butter, just like at the movies.

"Shhh," The three of us all said in unison. It was kind of nice that loving this show was the one thing we all had in common.

The opening scene depicted Suzanne lying in a hospital bed with a cast on her leg. "Where am I?" she asked. "How did I get here?"

19

DIRT

The next morning, it was as if Mom had forgotten all about the bonding we had done the night before. She was right back to being the enforcer of punishment. I tried ignoring her as I scooped my flavorless oatmeal into my mouth.

"Now remember, Paloma, you are going to be coming home right after school today," Mom said as she scraped the remaining bits of oatmeal from the pan and into the trash. "And I expect that you won't be doing any of those in-school readings. I don't want to be getting another call from your principal."

"But, Mom, there's this really cool plant club after school that I have been wanting to join," I said. "I swear it's super academic and boring. Plus, haven't you been telling me that you want me to get more involved with the school?"

I knew I had her there.

"You promise this is school related?" She looked at me with her suspicious gaze.

"Promise," I said honestly.

"Alright, you can go," Mom relented. "But make sure you come home right after. You have choir practice tonight."

If having to go to choir practice meant that I was allowed to go to DIRT, then I could live with that.

After messaging with Omar all night, we finally figured out a good time to do our reading! During our plant club of course! Aka my real reason for wanting to stay late after school today. Not that I wasn't excited to learn more about plants. As the newest member of the Drought Intolerant and Resistant Tree club or DIRT for short, I had the perfect excuse for needing to stay after school without Mom suspecting a thing!

Since it was after school hours, Barry said he would sit in on the reading for the first time, which I was excited about. Even though Barry had punched his last time clock years ago, he still never left a shift early. He had heard so much about my readings from the other students talking about them in the halls that he said he needed to see one for himself. It was nice to have an audience, even if it was just Barry and Dustin.

As soon as classes ended, Omar was waiting for me inside the greenhouse. He was as eager as I was to get things started, but I noticed he seemed a lot quieter than usual.

Willow, Thalia, and Fatima were currently setting up the audiovisual equipment for the reading. I still felt nervous being around Willow, knowing such a big secret about her family and worrying that her grandpa was lurking around somewhere to pressure me into telling her about her parents. I decided that I needed to stop worrying about Willow's grandpa and brought my focus back to setting up for Omar's reading. My backdrop of ivy and hanging flowers was already in position. It felt good to be out of the broom closet and back to the botanicals. We really pulled the place together in record time!

I pulled out my last remaining candle, which was already mostly used up from my reading with Jeremy, and set it up on the table. Since I was running low, I figured it wouldn't be such a bad thing for me to go to church group like Mom wanted. I needed to talk to a priest about replenishing my supply!

"I know you mentioned there was someone you were hoping to make contact with," I said. We had a whole text conversation about it, but he wouldn't give any hints about who he wanted to talk to!

"There is someone I have in mind," he said. He leaned back and crossed his arms.

"Ah," I said, recognizing his vagueness for skepticism. "So you don't exactly believe in this kind of thing, do you?"

Some skeptics thought that if they gave the name of a relative, the medium would fake speaking to them. As if!

"No, it's not that," Omar said. "I just don't want to interfere with the process or get my hopes up if the person I want to meet with doesn't come through."

I could understand that.

"Well—" I pressed the record button on my phone "—Omar Jackson of fifth period earth science, I hope we can channel just the right person you need to speak with."

I closed my eyes and began to concentrate. Within moments, swirls of flowers began to appear. When I opened my eyes, I couldn't believe what I was looking at: two Omars standing beside one another.

A chill went up my spine. I wasn't sure if it was due to a temperature change or a reaction from seeing double. One of the Omars was surrounded by tulips, the symbol for unconditional love, and the other had a translucent quality that I'd only ever seen in spirits. But that couldn't be possible. Omar couldn't be dead and alive at the same time.

I took off my glasses and rubbed my eyes, then returned the frames to my face. But the two Omars were still there.

"I'm sorry, Omar." I blinked extra hard as if that would somehow help. "I think there's something going on with my powers today."

"What do you mean?" Omar asked. "Is there something I can help with?"

"I'm not sure." I wiped my glasses on my shirt as if the second Omar might be a really detailed smudge that I could wipe away. "I'm seeing two of you."

His jaw dropped.

"That's my brother," he said. "I'm a twin. I don't think I've ever told anyone that at this school."

Fatima gasped, and Willow and Thalia looked equally as shocked. Normally, as the sound person, Fatima was the one to tell everyone else to be quiet on set. She quickly covered her mouth when she realized her mistake.

"Oh my gosh, Omar, I am so sorry. I don't know why I didn't think that was a possibility."

"My brother Okan passed away nearly three years ago." His voice wavered as he looked down at his shoes. "My parents up and moved my older sister and me from Indiana right after it happened. Something about needing a fresh start. I guess we took it to heart because neither of us talk about him with our new friends…" Omar trailed off. "Is that really you, Okan?"

I had no idea Omar was newer here and that he had been secretly dealing with this kind of grief by himself. I suddenly felt a wave of embarrassment for how much I had complained about moving.

"Yes, he's really here," I said. As I looked at Okan, I began to notice all of the little ways he was different from his twin. Even though Okan was three years younger, his confident posture gave off the impression of an older sibling. He was super translucent too, his brown skin was faded and I realized he might need a little extra assistance from the spirit mirror.

"Is there a message you would like me to pass on to your brother?" I spoke clearly into the spirit mirror's dark surface.

There was an immediate reply. *I want my brother to know I have always been by his side throughout his entire life, and I want him to know how proud I am of who he is. Tell him I always listen whenever he talks to me.*

I relayed the message to Omar, whose eyes were welling up with tears.

"I have always hoped he was with me." Omar wiped his cheek with his shirtsleeve. "Sometimes if I feel he might be there, I say things out loud just in case he can hear me. Every day feels a little emptier without him around, but knowing that he is with me makes me feel so much less alone."

I should really start bringing tissues to these things.

"Okan wants you to know that you never have to feel alone again and he will always be by your side rooting for you." Luckily, Willow had a packet of tissues from her bag, and she handed them to Omar.

"I think our time is almost up," I said. Okan was fading quickly.

"I love you, Okan." Omar somehow knew right where to look. I guess those twin intuitions were still strong even over the spectral plane.

After my reading with Omar ended, the question of what happened to Okan was behind all of our lips. But we shared the unspoken understanding that the more important question was to ask Omar how he was feeling.

"To be honest... I feel relieved," Omar said. "Okan will always be a part of who I am, and I was finally ready to share that with everyone here."

Before he left the greenhouse, Omar gave me a big hug, and Willow, Fatima, and Thalia joined in too.

"Thank you, Paloma. Really," he said on his way out the door. I had no idea that Omar was carrying around that grief, and I'm so happy that I was able to show him that Okan was always with him.

Being able to help Omar reminded me of why these readings were so important in the first place. They were meant to help people get closure by reconnecting with their loved ones. I had gotten so hung up on trying to impress Abuela so that she would take me with her on tour that I had started to lose sight of what these readings were really about. This wasn't supposed to be a way for me to impress anyone or make friends or look good to Abuela. This was about helping people. I was thankful for this reading with Omar to remind me of that.

After we parted ways with Omar, I helped Willow, Thalia, and Fatima put away the film club supplies in the closet down the hall. Willow lingered. She seemed like she had something she wanted to talk about. This was the first time we'd been alone together since her slumber party.

"Really awesome reading again today," Willow said. "It was so amazing that you were able to reconnect the brothers like that."

"Thanks," I said. "I seriously appreciate you all helping me as always. I think this was our best reading yet."

"I know this is a strange ask, but is it okay if I get your advice on something?" she said. Yellow carnations began popping out of her hair, the symbol for rejection and disappointment.

"Of course," I said, trying to hide my unease by forcing a smile.

"Well, you know how I told you all at the farmer's market that my parents have been fighting a lot lately?" She paused. "I guess what I'm trying to ask is, do you think you could get Dustin or one of the ghosts to spy on my parents and find out what they might be fighting about? I want to see if there is anything that I can do to help. Whenever I come into the room, they always stop and pretend like nothing happened. It's so odd."

I already had a pretty good guess at what they were fighting about.

"I don't know, Willow," I said. "I don't think it's a good idea to get ghosts to spy on your parents. Besides, I'm not sure if Barry or Dustin can actually leave the school since they're here all the time."

"What about the ghosts in my upstairs closet?" Willow beamed. "Do you think they could help?"

"Oh no...they're gone?" I said, reaching for an excuse. "They were just visiting."

"Well, I appreciate you for trying," Willow said.

"Uh, yeah. No problem," I said. My palms felt the clammiest they'd ever been. I hoped I didn't look too suspicious, like I knew something that I wasn't telling her. But there was no reason for her to think that. I needed to stop being so paranoid all the time.

I waved goodbye to Willow as I headed back to the greenhouse for the DIRT club meeting. For a second, I could have sworn I saw a glimpse of Willow's grandfather in the hallway...wherever Willow was, he never seemed to be far behind.

I checked my phone as I was walking to distract myself. Whoa, I had twelve new messages from Jasmin and Keisha!

KEISHA: Hey Paloma, sorry to bother you during school like this, but it's kind of an emergency.

JASMIN: Major emergency.

KEISHA: We need your help...like right away.

JASMIN: Preferably now if you can.

KEISHA: Call me.

I still had a few minutes before the club was going to start, so I ran over to the custodial closet and sat on a bucket that was still turned over from the last time I had been there.

"Hey," I said as soon as Keisha picked up the phone. "What's going on?"

"It's Eloise," Keisha said, her voice shaking. "She's missing."

"What do you mean, she's missing?" I asked. "You mean she ran away or something?"

"We've looked everywhere!" Keisha's sobs were muffled through the phone, but I could definitely tell she was crying. "We checked all her usual spots. I think she's gone forever."

"Okay," I said in my calmest voice possible. "How can I help?"

"Can't you find her with your powers?" Keisha said.

"They don't exactly work like that." I scrambled, trying to think of a solution. "Let me try something for a second."

I closed my eyes and started to meditate, hoping for a flower premonition. Swirls of zinnia, the flower for absent friends, appeared in the air. Not the most helpful since we already knew this, but at least it validated that Eloise was actually lost.

"Okay, so she is definitely lost," I said. "But I'm not sure what else I can do. I'm not going to be much use to you guys and your search party all the way out here in California."

I felt totally helpless.

"Don't you have an uncle or something that deals with this kind of thing though?" Keisha asked.

"You mean my uncles Raul and Julian?" I asked. "I guess I could try them on the spirit mirror and see if they finished their mission tracking down their friend's ferret in Texas."

Though if they had this much trouble finding a ferret, I couldn't imagine how they were going to find a missing human being. They were animal psychics after all. I wasn't exactly sure they would be able to help, but it was worth a shot. I didn't want to let Jasmine and Keisha down.

"I'll see what I can do," I said. "Look, I've got to go. But I'll try to get in touch with my uncles to see if they can help out with your friend."

I hung up the phone before Keisha could reply. Barry the hall monitor appeared through the door, tapping his imaginary watch furiously.

"Yes, yes, I know. I'm going." I picked up my bag and sprinted to DIRT club. I made it just in time.

Normally, learning new botanical facts was something

I was super into, but with Eloise's disappearance, I just couldn't focus. Jasmin and Keisha needed me—they were really upset! Keisha was not a crier, so to hear her like that on the phone meant this situation was seriously bad. Even if Eloise was replacing me as a friend, I didn't want her to be missing!

As soon as I got a free moment, I sent the message to my uncles explaining the situation.

Hi, Uncle Raul! Hi, Uncle Julian! Hope everything is going well on your ferret search. If you can, I was wondering if you could do me a favor. My best friends, Jasmin and Keisha, need help finding their friend Eloise who went missing today. Do you think you can help? I don't know what else to do.

I got a reply with the words I wanted to hear: *We're on the case.*

Wow, that was easy. I sent another message: *Do you need me to find out any more details for you?*

We've got it from here. Thanks for reaching out. No need to stress any further! We will find Eloise.

I let Jasmin and Keisha know that my uncles were on it. Hopefully that would help them to feel a little better.

Now that the pressure of finding a missing person was

off my plate, I was able to focus my attention on planning for my next reading, which involved acquiring candles. And I knew just the way to do it.

20

Crickets

When I got home after the DIRT club meeting, Mom was ready with her reminder that I had choir practice tonight.

"Don't get too comfortable. We have to leave as soon as your sister gets home," she said the second I sat down on the couch.

Guess there would be no relaxing for me today!

My candle stash was completely empty after Omar's reading, so I didn't actually mind going. If there was one place in the world that I knew carried blessed candles, it was church.

"Try not to think of it as a punishment," Mom said, which only made it feel more like it was supposed to be a punishment.

"If you say so," I said in my most monotone voice possible. If I seemed too eager to go, she'd know something was up.

"There's going to be tons of girls there your age," she said as if somehow that would make going seem less bad. "And you'll even have your sister with you."

She ruffled the back of my head which was currently buried in a couch cushion.

Sure, Magdalena and I have been getting along a little better ever since our talk the other night about her having powers, but was she completely trustworthy? Guess I'd find out soon enough.

"Why is Magdalena being punished too?" I wondered if Mom had found out about her TikTok account.

"Again, not a punishment." She tried extra hard to sound convincing.

As soon as Magdalena got home, we set off for Our Lady of Mount Carmel, a tall white building with large wooden doors and a bell tower that loomed at the top of the structure. As soon as the clock struck 5:00 p.m., the bell began to sway back and forth, playing the familiar deep hollow melody of "We Gather Together," which echoed in the open landscape. Once inside, we were instructed by one of the choir moms to head upstairs to the loft where there were about thirty other girls already seated around the organ. At least I wasn't the oldest one here like I had been at my last choir back in Miami.

"Ah, I see our two new members have finally arrived," a woman with black frizzy curls cooed. "I'm Ms. Rizzo, the choir director." Her paisley shawl draped around her short plump frame, which made it seem more like a blanket than anything else.

"Nice to meet you," Magdalena and I said as we took our seats in the back, near the soprano IIs.

"And beside me is Mr. Capobianco, the organist." Ms. Rizzo gestured to a man in a dress shirt with dark slicked-back hair sitting at the organ bench. He had the kind of perfect posture that would have made Lucy Lammermoor happy. Everything about him seemed super polished, minus the fact that he wasn't wearing any shoes, which made me wonder if it had something to do with keeping the organ pedals clean.

Magdalena and I gave another awkward wave.

"Before we dive into the music, there is something I want you all to remember," Ms. Rizzo said. "God doesn't hear the sounds of our voices, he hears the sounds of our hearts."

Although I would imagine that Ms. Rizzo must care a little bit about how we sounded.

The warm-ups were kind of hard to get the hang of since they were mostly comprised of complicated tongue twisters, but once we got to the actual music, I recognized some of my favorites like "All This Bright and Beautiful" and "Panis Angelicus." It was always more fun to sing when you already knew the words.

After rehearsal was over, we were instructed to head to the sacristy to try on our new robes. They were long and purple with a white V-shaped neck covering. At least they were slightly better than the little red gowns my last choir made us wear.

I was about to make a joke to Magdalena about how ridiculous we must look until I realized she was nowhere to be seen.

I was almost in full panic mode until I spotted her head sticking out of a set of purple robes that were ten sizes too large as she shuffled back into the room. The sleeves hung loosely at her sides.

"Where have you been hiding?" I scolded. "You definitely weren't in here a minute ago."

"Just exploring." She squirmed, her cheeks turning

bright pink, like she was suppressing a laugh. I didn't have to wonder for long what she was up to. A familiar chirping sound rang out from under her robes.

She'd brought the crickets.

"You've got to be kidding me." I rolled my head backward. "Magdalena, don't do it!"

"I thought you wanted us to get kicked out of choir," she said.

"When did I ever say that?" I asked.

"You didn't have to! I could tell through the bonds of sisterhood." She smiled.

Another chirp.

"I didn't want to join choir, but that doesn't mean I want to get kicked out of it either! Mom is going to kill us if she finds out about this." I looked around the room to make sure no one was watching at us. "Magdalena, we are going to get in so much trouble. You need to get rid of the crickets. Those are for your gecko, Chorizo, not for pranking."

"My mistake. That's on me. I read the situation completely wrong. Not to worry though, I can fix this. Be right back!" She slowly and discreetly snuck outside, returning moments later.

Crisis averted. Or so I thought.

It turned out the crickets followed Magdalena back down the stairs and into the rehearsal room. Half the choir was now running around and screaming, trying to get away from the swarm of jumping bugs. Luckily, there was no way this was going to get traced back to us. It's not like anyone saw Magdalena with the crickets besides me. Plus, in the midst of the chaos, I was able to grab some candles that were lying out on the table, which saved me the stress of having to ask. So, that was a success.

Abuela said that it was important to get permission from the priest, but I didn't have time with all of the cricket chaos to find a priest and explain to him what I was up to. Most priests weren't cool with séances, so I didn't want to take the chance that he'd say no.

"Where do you think you're going with those?" a thunderous voice asked.

I turned around to find myself looking at a priest. But not just any priest—this was the spirit of a priest. He could have passed for someone alive if it weren't for the fact that he was hovering several inches off the ground and that he was wearing his purple vestments when it wasn't even Advent yet!

"I…uh…" I tried coming up with a good excuse but decided to confess, since that's what you were supposed to do around priests anyway. "I need these for a spirit reading that I'm doing."

"A spirit reading, huh? You really shouldn't be using these tools to summon anything," he said sternly. "You are messing with things that you shouldn't be messing with. The church takes a firm stance against divination."

"I know, I know," I sighed. Mom reminded me of this all the time. "But this is different. I'm not trying to summon anything bad. I'm trying to help people reconnect with their loved ones so they can move on. It's kind of a family business."

"Look," the priest put his hands together in prayer. A set of wooden rosaries hung from his wrist. "I don't believe that seeing and speaking to ghosts is a bad thing, but seeking out these conversations can be dangerous. Once you open that door to these unsafe interactions, it is hard to close it."

He didn't need to rub it in. I had already dealt with a school full of ghosts.

"That's why I need the candles," I explained.

"Alright, my child, look." He seemed like he was having

an existential crisis between wanting to help and wanting me to stop talking to ghosts. Which was funny, considering I was talking to him and he was a ghost. "I will give you my blessing to take these since it sounds like you are only looking to get protection, but I urge you to consider perhaps not doing these readings."

"Thank you for letting me have the candles, Father... uh," I said.

"Father McNamara," he replied before floating in the direction of the rectory.

I did feel way less guilty now that I got permission from a priest, even if he was a ghost priest, but I made a note to check in with one that was alive the next time I had to go to choir practice.

The crickets had finally found their way out of the church thanks to Ms. Rizzo shooing them all out of the space with a missalette while the rest of the girls continued running around and screaming. Mr. Capobianco kept playing the organ as if nothing were happening at all.

As I lay in bed that night, I felt a sense of accomplishment. I was able to reason with the unreasonable Magdalena, and I got a new supply of blessed candles from the church! Today was a good day…until I felt something crawl across my leg.

Chirp.

I knew exactly what this was. The crickets!

"Magdalena!"

21

Double Trouble

Another day, another reading. I told Maryam from third period social studies that I would meet her in my usual spot in the greenhouse. The only issue was, I was running late. By the time I got to the greenhouse, Maryam was sitting at one of the benches tapping her finger against her arm.

"What took you so long?" She had been waiting for a little over ten minutes, which in school time was like an eternity.

"I'm sorry," I said. "We had to track down the key to the film club's equipment closet."

Things were already off to a rocky start between me

and Maryam, but they got even rockier when the room began to shake much more than usual, causing the candles to fall over onto the table which started a small fire. I quickly patted it out before it spread further on the tablecloth. This was not a good way to start.

The spirit that came through had her mouth twisted in the same scowl that Maryam currently wore. Since she was about my height at five-two, I could feel her cold breath right against my face. She had on a cranberry-colored pantsuit with a large gold bracelet that dangled against her light brown skin.

Oreo the cat, who had been comfortably perched on Dustin's head, was startled by the sound of the spirit's jewelry rattling together. He dug his claws deeper into Dustin, who was now trying to wrestle Oreo off himself.

"Who are you?" the woman called out.

"I'm just someone who is here to help you talk to Maryam," I explained.

"I can talk to her just fine without you," the spirit huffed.

"I'm not so sure that you can. She won't be able to hear you." I gestured to Maryam who seemed disinterested by my half of the conversation and was now scrolling through her phone.

"We'll see about that," the spirit replied. "Maryam, darling," she shouted in a loud loving tone. "It's me, your Auntie Bibi."

Maryam was now looking at me, waiting for me to do something.

I explained that her aunt came through for her, but before I could get through my first sentence, the spirit snapped at me.

"I don't need your help!" Auntie Bibi interjected. "Just let me talk to my niece. This is a private conversation."

She turned away from me and floated closer to Maryam, speaking louder and louder with each word.

This was going nowhere.

"I think I have an idea." I placed the spirit mirror on the table.

I didn't want Maryam's auntie to feel upset at the fact that she couldn't do things on her own, but maybe the spirit mirror could help!

"What is this?" Maryam inspected the compact.

"Yes, please explain." Auntie Bibi's words appeared on its surface.

"This will allow you to talk to your auntie without me having to translate. You will be able to see her responses appear right there." I pointed to where Auntie Bibi's words were, hoping it would work for her like it always did for me.

I stopped the live stream to respect Maryam's aunt's wishes about wanting privacy.

Willow nodded and closed out of the app.

"I'll leave you to it then," I said to Maryam.

The rest of us walked to the other side of the greenhouse to give them some space. Willow, Thalia, and Fatima decided to work on their homework at one of the tables while I chose to sit at the table closest to Dustin, who was floating on top of a sculpted topiary.

"What do you think they're talking about?" Dustin asked.

"Who knows." I shrugged. "I always try to remember that the healing process is a two-way street and that maybe Maryam's auntie needs some closure just as much as she does."

"Makes sense," Dustin said. "Speaking of healing, how have things been at home with getting your mom to be okay with you talking to ghosts?"

"Still pretty much the same." I cradled my face between my hands on the table. "Except now my sister and I have gotten closer ever since I found out she has powers. Although, I'm a little bummed out that I'm not the only one who gets extra special medium advice from Abuela anymore."

He sat across from me at the table with Oreo in his lap. "You're both new at this, and it's really special that you can experience all these things together. Plus, I've been watching almost all of your readings since you got here and you've definitely improved a ton. You can help her like nobody else can."

Oreo climbed back on top of his head.

"Thanks, Dustin." I guess I was getting better at this!

I checked my phone. Lunch would be over in a few minutes, and we still needed to wrap this reading up. I ran back over to Maryam and her auntie.

"I hate to interrupt you two," I whispered.

"I know, lunch is almost over." Maryam smiled. "I can't believe how fast the time flew. Thank you, Paloma, for helping me speak to my auntie. That spirit mirror is really cool."

She seemed way less annoyed at me than she had been earlier.

"It is, isn't it?" I smiled, happy to hear that her interaction went well and that the spirit mirror worked.

"I know we got off to the wrong foot earlier," Auntie Bibi said, hovering closer to me. "You aren't so bad after all. I had a very good chat with my niece."

I nodded as I pocketed the spirit mirror.

It was time to close the portal. I closed my eyes and concentrated, causing the room to shake almost as violently as it did when Auntie Bibi first arrived. I held on to the base of the candles this time so they wouldn't fall over again. The indoor palm trees swayed like they were in a tropical storm. Then there was calmness again and everything looked as normal as if nothing had happened at all. The air warmed up and Auntie Bibi was successfully back on the other side of the spirit realm. I blew out the candles and packed up my supplies.

"I'm so happy I got to know more about my auntie," Maryam said. "She died saving my life in a car crash when I was super little. It was nice to be able to thank her for what she did for me."

I came prepared with tissues this time and handed her a packet from my backpack. Seeing Maryam interact with her auntie made me think of my aunts and uncles back home and how much I missed them. I wondered if Aunt Maria was still coming home late from her appointments analyzing people's dreams, or if Aunt Rosa and Uncle Esteban were still having their nightly arguments about whether star charts were more accurate than numerology predictions. Homesickness was beginning to set in hard.

Maryam and I said our goodbyes and I power walked to my next class. I didn't want her to see that I was starting to get upset. I was a professional after all.

When I finally arrived to social studies class, late of course and out of breath, my jaw practically hit the floor.

The entire room was filled with ghosts in marching band uniforms, and more seemed to be piling into the room by the second.

I guess I should have addressed getting the rest of the ghosts out of the school and closing the spirit portal in the cafeteria for good when I had the chance… It didn't seem like as big of an issue at the time. Especially since I had gotten most of them out and I didn't have the time to go searching for the stragglers, but there was no ignoring this now.

To make matters worse, my powers were freaking out again from the overstimulation, which caused flowers to pop up everywhere. Between the ghosts and the flowers, I could barely make out the path to my desk.

I needed to get out of here. I ran back into the hallway as the bell was ringing. I knew Mom would ground me for a million years once she found out what I'd done, but this was a psychic emergency. The hallway, which was empty of any spirit activity a moment ago, was now flooded with ghosts. I recognized a lot of them as the ones I thought I sent back through the first time. Except this time, they weren't as transparent looking, which meant they'd have more energy to cause mayhem. And from what I could tell, they were already wreaking havoc in the school. A group of the marching band students swung from the light fixtures, causing them to rock back and forth, while the squad of Girl Scouts ran down the halls ripping posters off the walls.

This was bad. Really, really bad.

The only person who could help me now was Abuela and that meant admitting what I'd done. But I didn't exactly have any other choice. She was the only person who would know what to do in this situation. I reached for my spirit mirror and sent her a message.

Abuela—help! My school is overrun by ghosts, what should I do?

Abuela was normally pretty good at getting back to

me whenever I had medium-related questions, but after a few minutes of not hearing anything back, I opted for plan B and called the landline in Miami.

The phone rang a few times before I heard the click of someone picking up on the other end.

"Abuela?" I said eagerly.

"Paloma, is that you?" It was Aunt Rosa.

"Hi, Aunt Rosa," I said. "Is Abuela there? I kind of have an important question to ask her."

"I'm sorry, sweetie," Aunt Rosa replied. "Abuela is on tour right now in South America. I think this week she's supposed to be in Argentina…or was it Peru? It's so hard to keep track of her schedule. Did you try her on the spirit mirror?"

Oh no, the tour! My heart sank at the realization that she left without me. This was way ahead of schedule too. Even though I got rid of my tour countdown clock, I thought I still had time!

Abuela was famous for pretty much going off the grid when she went on tour, so it was going to be almost impossible to get in touch with her, and I really needed her now more than ever.

"I already tried the spirit mirror." I sighed. "When is she supposed to be back?"

"Not for another few weeks at least. Definitely before Christmas," Aunt Rosa said. "Is this something I could possibly be able to help you with?"

Even if she could help, I didn't want to tell her about my mistake and risk it getting back to Mom.

"No, that's okay," I said. "It can wait."

"Alright, well, if you're sure," Aunt Rosa said.

"Thanks anyway." I hung up.

I was on my own.

First things first, I needed to track down this portal and fast. The school was at maximum ghost capacity. And to make matters worse, I ran into Willow who was currently being flanked by her grandfather.

"Not you again," I groaned. He was the last person I wanted to see right now.

"Um, okay hi. Nice to see you too," Willow said, looking hurt.

"I'm sorry." I closed my eyes as if that was somehow going to make the sound of a hundred ghosts talking more bearable. "I am seeing every ghost that's ever walked the planet right now and it's kind of a lot. All the ghosts that we thought we got rid of are back."

"Oh… That's not good." Willow bit her lip. "Do you think you can fix it like last time?"

"I don't know." I took a few steps away from her toward the greenhouse. Yellow carnations zoomed across the room. "I should be able to officially seal it shut this time now that I am fully restocked on my candle supply."

"What about the divorce?" her grandfather shouted at me. "You didn't tell her about the divorce! I need you to tell her. I need her to stop it. You have to help!"

I stopped in my tracks, my whole body tense as a spring. One problem at a time! But ignoring her grandfather was getting harder by the minute. He was too persistent.

"Not now," I muttered under my breath as I waved my arm in his direction to shoo him away.

"What was that?" Willow asked.

"Nothing," I said, "just ghosts again."

I paused for a second to think. Maybe if I told Willow the truth, her grandfather's ghost would leave me alone and then I could focus on getting the rest of the ghosts out of here before they caused any more damage. At least that would solve one problem.

After finding out about what happened to Suzanne La

Luca, I couldn't help but think that if Abuela had warned her, she wouldn't have gotten into that accident in the first place. Maybe it was better for people to get all messages from the spirits. Maybe the rules were wrong. Or at least worth breaking depending on the circumstance.

I decided to go for it.

"There's actually something that I need to tell you, Willow. It's your grandfather. He's sort of been following you around ever since your party." I gestured to the ghost standing behind her that I knew she couldn't see. "He's been wanting me to tell you something this whole time, but I didn't want to because I thought it would make you upset. But who am I to decide what will and won't make you upset? Also, your grandpa won't leave me alone about it, and it might be the only way to get him to cross over if I tell you."

"It sounds like you should probably tell me then if he really wants me to know that badly," she said matter-of-factly.

See, it really was that simple!

"Okay, well, I should start out by saying this is probably going to be difficult to hear." I wanted her to mentally prepare herself for what I was about to reveal.

"Yeah, of course," she said.

I already made up my mind so there was no second-guessing myself now! Telling her would be the honest thing to do, so this was definitely what I should be doing, right?

"Okay, there's no easy way to say this, but…your parents are getting divorced." I felt a rush of relief that I was finally able to get that off my chest.

But Willow's face went stone-cold.

"You're lying," she said.

The sudden chill I felt in the room wasn't from the ghosts. It was from the feeling of all the blood draining from my body at the look Willow was giving me right now.

"What? No." My stomach felt like it was doing backflips. "You said you wanted me to tell you. And your grandpa was the one who put me up to this!"

This wasn't going well. I tried looking over to her grandfather for backup, but he had already disappeared. Coward.

"You're just trying to make me feel bad." She took a few steps back.

"That's not what I'm doing, I swear," I said.

"This is so messed up." She held her hand up to signal

me to stop talking. "I can't believe I thought you were my friend. Don't talk to me anymore."

I stood in place, completely stunned. Before I could say anything else, Willow was already storming off into a sea of ghosts, leaving a trail of petunias in her wake, the symbol for anger. And despite the hundreds of ghosts that were now standing around me, I felt more alone than ever.

22

The Necklace

My new best friend hated me, Abuela left for tour without me, and now I was going to have to face the wrath of Mom for skipping class. And there was still the issue of my school being overrun by ghosts. Could today get any worse? Apparently it could.

"So, I bet you know who I was on the phone with today," Mom's voice bellowed as soon as I stepped foot in the door. I had a feeling that my bad day was only just the beginning. She was holding her phone so tight that I was afraid the screen was going to shatter into tiny little pieces in her hands.

I wasn't sure if this was one of those questions you weren't supposed to answer.

"The principal," Mom said, her knuckles white. "You skipped class today and have been issued a detention. And do you know who I spoke to after that?"

"No?" Am I supposed to be answering these?

"Willow's dad," she said matter-of-factly. "Do you know why he called?"

Oh no.

"Well," she clicked her tongue. "A very angry Mr. Goldstein informed me that you told Willow that he and his wife were getting divorced. Why would you think it was okay to say something like that? And where did you even get that kind of information?"

"But I didn't…" I was barely able to finish the last word before she cut me off.

"Even if you were right, which you were, what have I told you about using your powers? The Goldsteins weren't planning to tell Willow the news until after the new year, and they were completely unprepared."

At least she wasn't shouting anymore.

"Her grandfather made me do it." The words blurted out of my mouth as my eyes welled up with tears. "I didn't want to say anything but he wouldn't leave me alone about it. And then all these other ghosts started showing up and it all just got so out of hand, I didn't know what to do."

Interacting with a school full of ghosts and getting into a fight with my best friend in California was too much to deal with in a single day. I couldn't hold back the floodgate of my emotions for a second longer.

"Explain," Mom demanded. There was a hint of sympathy in her tone, which was unusual for her when she was this angry.

She needed to know that this wasn't completely my fault. Plus, I was out of options for how I was going to fix this. I was already in trouble, so what did I have to lose? Maybe Mom would go lighter on the punishments if she knew I was being peer pressured by a ghost. Even if Mom didn't have any powers, she might know how to help. At least I hoped so.

Everything I had been hiding from her for the past few months came spilling out of me like water escaping from a broken dam. I told her what went down at Willow's birthday party, how I had used the Ouija board even though I knew it was against the rules, and how I ended up accidentally opening up the spirit portal for more ghosts to come through. I told her all of it. All the information I had been trying to hide from her this entire time escaped from my mouth. Because it was all so overwhelming, getting this off my chest actually felt like a weight had been lifted off me.

"Her grandpa kept telling me to tell Willow because he thought it would help to save her parent's marriage." I was hyperventilating through my tears. "I didn't know what to do and I couldn't get in touch with Abuela. I was so burned-out from having to fix everything and then—" I sobbed. "I thought I was helping, but I just made everything worse!"

"Okay, I think I'm getting the picture." Mom let out a long sigh and held my hand as we sat together on the couch. "I wish this is something you felt like you could come to me with. I could have helped you with this sooner if you had just told me what was going on. But I guess I haven't made it easy for you." She paused. "There's something I've been keeping from you girls."

She was definitely still mad, but I think part of her felt bad for me. At least I'd hoped so.

Mom continued. "I figured I'd have to tell you this one

of these days, and maybe if I had told you sooner, this wouldn't have happened."

"Tell me what?" I asked. I clenched a pillow against my body for support.

"I want to know too!" Magdalena came running into the room from the kitchen where she was clearly eavesdropping.

Mom patted the seat next to her on the couch. "You know how you girls got those amethyst jewelry pieces from your Aunt Rosa? And how everyone in our family wears one?"

Magdalena and I both nodded.

"Well…" She paused to take a deep inhale. "That's because I have the gift."

"What?" I blinked heavily as I tried to process this information. I was completely stunned. "But you hate ghosts. You're always saying how you don't want me talking to them. You're telling me you've had powers this whole time?"

Surely she had to be talking about a different kind of gift. The kind that actually came wrapped up in a box and not the powers kind. My brain was rejecting this information as fast as it was coming in. What the heck was going on today?

"I came into my powers when I was your age," she said. Her neck was strained with tension as she spoke, but not the angry kind. "And, like you, I wanted to be the greatest medium of all time, just like my mom. But then things happened that made me start to dislike my abilities. You see, in addition to being able to see and speak to ghosts, I am also a mind reader, which is a very complicated gift to have. I was constantly learning information that I did not want to know and over the years I was able to adopt different techniques to stifle my abilities. With the help of your aunts and uncles, we eventually figured out that amethyst, being a protection stone, was the most effective blocker of my powers."

So that's how she always knew what I was up to! Very creepy.

"Yes," she said. "I know, it's very creepy."

I touched my neck and panicked at the realization that I wasn't wearing my necklace.

"Like your situation with Willow, I ended up finding things out about people that they wouldn't want me to know. And it was upsetting to learn what others thought about me. It got so bad that eventually I started to hate my gift. When I was in high school, I had a really close group of friends. I thought we all got along so well, but they didn't know about my powers and I wanted to keep it that way. I didn't want them to feel afraid to think freely around me and I really tried my best not to read their minds. But sometimes people's thoughts are so loud that they just come through."

"So, what happened?" I asked.

Magdalena and I were on the edges of our seats.

"Well, I found out the hard way that my friends weren't really as nice as I thought they were. In fact, it turned out they didn't even like me at all. I was devastated. I tried pretending like things were normal, but one day my emotions got the better of me and I called them out on it. They were stunned and never wanted to speak to me again after that. Instead of apologizing and confronting the situation, I made your abuela send me to a private Catholic school where I learned techniques to suppress my gift even more. I never wanted to use my powers again."

I felt bad for Mom, but now that I knew all this, maybe she would be able to help me with my problems after all.

"So what do you think I should do to try to get Willow back? And what about the spirit portal?" I asked.

I pictured poor Barry and Dustin, trapped in a school full of ghosts.

"I am going to see if I can get in touch with your grandmother," she said. "We will figure this out…together."

"I thought she was off the grid," I said.

"Don't worry. I have special ways of reaching her." She tapped her forehead.

I went with Magdalena to my room while I waited for Mom to get a hold of Abuela.

"Want to tell us what's wrong, button?" Harrison appeared outside my window.

He really needed to stop calling me that. Beryl was not far behind him.

I filled them in on the whole situation.

"I know you made a mistake, but beating yourself up like this isn't going to make things any better," Beryl said.

"Maybe I shouldn't even have this gift in the first place. Maybe Mom was right all along and I should suppress my powers. Talking to ghosts only leads to trouble," I said. "Maybe the dead are supposed to stay gone."

"Whoa, let's not get too carried away there." Beryl crossed her arms over her chest. "Look, it sounds like this whole situation got out of control, but there are ways of fixing friendships even when things get really bad."

"There's no fixing this." I buried my face in my knees. "Willow is going to hate me forever. I ruined her family."

I just wanted to disappear or get amnesia like Suzanne La Luca and forget all of this ever happened.

"Willow's grandpop really put a lot of pressure on you to tell her about her parents," Harrison said. "That wasn't his call to make. And it was wrong of him to think a kid could fix that kind of situation anyway."

"He was very insistent about it." I held back the urge to blow my nose. I wish I hadn't brought all of my tissue packs to school.

There was a knock at my door.

"Paloma," Mom cooed as she pushed the door open a crack. "I have Abuela on the phone."

"Abuela!" My heart brightened.

If anyone knew what to do, it was going to be her. I ran toward Mom and snatched the phone out of her hands. Abuela's face was big against the screen.

"I thought you left your phone in Miami!" I was so excited to see her again.

"Your mom has her ways of reaching me." Abuela

winked. "And one of my crew members was nice enough to let me borrow their phone. It sounds to me like you're in a bit of a pickle."

That was an understatement. This was Paloma's one hundred flavors of pickle problems.

"I got myself into this mess trying to impress you enough so you would want to take me with you on tour." I frowned. "I was doing so well, too, until I ended up breaking the rules and using a Ouija board at Willow's party. And now there's a spirit portal open at school that I can't seem to get rid of! How do I fix this?"

"Well, I will tell you what your first mistake was, darling, and I am not talking about the Ouija board. You were doing the readings for personal gain. Remember, the whole point is to help people. Once that gets cast aside, you open yourself up to all kinds of trouble. And speaking of that, you need to be honest and apologize to your friend," Abuela said. "I hope you realize now why we have these rules in place for not telling people everything the spirits of their loved ones have to say. Sometimes you need to let people experience the events in their life. Knowing the future, especially when there is nothing you can do to change it, isn't much good to anyone."

"I guess you're right," I sighed. "What if Willow doesn't accept my apology? And what if I can't close the spirit portal for good?"

"The spirit portal will close once you've resolved your issues with your friend," Abuela said. "Stress and anxiety can be pretty powerful. You need to be in a calm meditative state to close the portal and the only way you will be able to get there is if you make up with Willow. The only person that can close a portal is the person who opened it. But I have complete faith in you, my dear."

"Great, no pressure." It felt like every muscle in my body had turned to jelly.

"These powers come with a lot of responsibility," Abuela said, "which is why it is so important that we follow a strict set of rules to try to prevent things like this from happening. Remember what I always tell you about mistakes, darling? It's how we learn and grow. I'm pretty sure you won't be doing something like this again in the future, right?"

"Right," I grumbled.

"See," Abuela said. "All part of the growing experience."

I could feel the tightness in my chest slowly ease away.

"And in the future, if you can't get in touch with me to talk about something, you should really think about going to your mom. She understands your situation more than you'd think. Te amo, Paloma." And with that Abuela ended our call.

"Get any good tips from your grandma?" Mom held her hand out for me to return her phone.

"I sure did," I said as I put my amethyst necklace around my neck to block out Mom's mind reading. "And I'm going to need Magdalena's help. This calls for the bonds of sisterhood."

23

Bonds of Sisterhood

Operation: Get Willow Back was going to be harder than I had expected. It turned out Thalia and Fatima were giving me the silent treatment as well, which meant getting them on board to help me was now off the table.

"Come on," I pleaded, leaning against Thalia's locker. "I really need your help with this. It's not going to work without you."

"What's not going to work?" Thalia said. Fatima elbowed her in the ribs for breaking the silent treatment. "What? I want to know!"

"I can prove it that I'm not making it up!" I said.

"So you're saying Willow's grandpa really put you up

to this?" Thalia closed her locker. "How do we know if we can believe you?"

"That's the beauty of it." I beamed. "You don't have to believe me! My sister can videotape ghosts. So if I do a reading for Willow, she will see that it was really her grandpa who wanted her to know this information. It'll be like the reading we did for Maryam, only better because she will actually be able to see her grandpa!"

"And you're sure this is going to work?" Fatima asked.

"It has to." There were definitely a lot of variables involved, which included getting Willow to meet with me and hoping that her grandpa would show up, but this was a risk that I had take.

I needed it to work.

Since Abuela gave Magdalena her own spirit mirror a few weeks ago, I messaged Magdalena on it that Operation: Get Willow Back was a go.

Meet me at the middle school when you're done with classes for the day. I need you to work your spirit photography magic.

She replied:

I thought you'd never ask.

Thankfully the local elementary school was only a few

blocks away so it wouldn't be an issue for her to get here after school was over.

I coordinated with Thalia and Fatima to have Willow show up at the greenhouse after school. I had the room already set up for the reading before last period was over. Everything was perfect. All I needed was Willow to be there.

Magdalena arrived early and was already using her phone to communicate with Barry and Dustin in the greenhouse while we waited. Her followers were loving the new ghost content.

With every second that ticked by, I was starting to worry that Willow wasn't going to come. That was until I heard the squeaking of her sneakers coming down the hallway. Thank goodness Thalia and Fatima came through.

Willow entered the greenhouse with them on either side of her.

"Wait a minute." Her cheeks turned beet red. "What are we doing here? I told you I didn't want to talk to her anymore."

Fatima had her elbow locked with Willow's to keep her from running off.

"Paloma has something she wants to show you, and I think you're going to want to see it."

"She wants to try to channel your grandfather using her sister's camera powers so she can prove that he wanted you to know about your parents," Thalia added.

Willow started to squirm, but then stopped. "Wait, you're saying I could *see* him?"

"Yes," I replied.

Willow still looked skeptical, but she eventually said, "Okay, you have one chance."

I breathed out a sigh of relief.

"Great! Let's do this then." I gestured for Magdalena to join me. She had gotten distracted following Dustin around with her phone's camera.

I wasn't sure I could reason with the universe, but just in case, I hoped it was feeling generous today. I lit my candles, closed my eyes, and began to concentrate more than I had ever concentrated in my entire life. I'd never tried to call upon a specific spirit before, so this was new to me. After a few moments, the room began to shake and the temperature dropped, which meant that someone had come through.

"It's working, its working!" Magdalena shouted. "I can

see an old man on my camera! This must be the grandpa you were talking about."

Her camera was pointed toward me and Willow, who had reluctantly taken a seat across from me. Three small flickering candles sat between us. Magdalena turned her phone so that Willow could see what she was talking about. A look of recognition came over Willow's face.

I couldn't believe this was actually working. I put the spirit mirror on the table in front of her.

"This will show you exactly what your grandfather is saying, just like Maryam's reading," I said.

I was going to prove once and for all to her that I was telling the truth! Magdalena held out her phone for Willow to see the image of her grandpa's spirit.

"Pop pop!" Willow held her hands against her chest. "It really is you!"

He glided closer to where Willow was currently sitting.

"Willow's grandpa," I said. "I need you to tell Willow what you told me at the party."

"No," he said stubbornly and folded his arms. "I don't want her to be mad at me."

"What do you mean you don't want her to be mad at

you!" I shouted. "That's not fair that she gets to be mad at me when you're the one who caused this!"

"You didn't have to tell her what I told you." He frowned.

"Oh, is that so?" I sounded like Mom when she was scolding me. "Because you made it sound like it was pretty urgent."

"Yeah, but I didn't know she was going to react that way." He floated even closer to his granddaughter. Magdalena was getting it all on camera and the spirit mirror was picking up everything he was saying.

"Can you ask him why he thought me knowing this was going to help?" Willow asked.

Her grandfather looked stunned. "She can hear me?"

"Yes," I replied, feeling pretty smug that I had tricked him into a confession. "She knows everything you just said."

My impulse to gloat was immediately ruined by the spirit of her grandfather breaking into tears. I'd never made a spirit cry before and it did not feel great.

"Willow, I am so sorry about everything," he said. "All I wanted was to try to help fix your parents' marriage, and I thought you would be able to convince them to stay together. Can you find it in your heart to forgive an old ghost like me?"

Tears began to well up in Willow's eyes too. "Of course I forgive you."

"I'm sorry too, Willow," I said. "I should have known better than to share that message with you. That wasn't fair of me."

"I forgive you both." Willow wrapped her arms around me in a hug. "I'm sorry that I called you a liar. I just didn't want what you were saying to be true. It's not your fault this happened."

"I should have been more considerate of your feelings." I pulled away from the hug to look at her face. "Friends again?"

Willow smiled. "Friends again."

Now that I had made up with Willow, I shut my eyes and concentrated on closing the portal to the spirit world. I emptied my thoughts, letting the warmth of my repaired friendship spread through me. In order to send Willow's grandpa and the rest of the ghosts that occupied the school back through, I had to focus extra hard, like Abuela said. But if I could fix things with Willow, I could do anything.

The room suddenly shook more violently than usual, knocking us all to the ground. The hanging baskets swayed and tumbled to the floor. But then, everything was still and quiet.

"What was that?" Thalia said as she used a large planter to brace herself.

"Spirit portal," I said. "All that ghost activity shook things up a little more than usual."

I felt relieved that the ghosts were gone, except for Barry and Dustin and Oreo of course. Barry was going to be so relieved.

Magdalena came over beside me, looking out of the window through her phone. "You really saved the day with your spirit photography skills," I said. "I owe you one."

She smiled and bumped her shoulder with mine. "Nah. What else are the bonds of sisterhood for?"

24

Lost and Found

Now that I wasn't distracted from the million stray ghosts wandering around, I decided to try another self-prediction once I was back in the safety of my room. I needed to find out if everything was truly back to normal.

I opened my journal and tried to think of a good question to ask and there was only one that was coming to mind.

Will there be any more drama this year?

White poppy, the symbol for renewal, lavender, the symbol for tranquility, and crocus, the symbol for new beginnings, danced around the page.

Phew! A positive prediction. That was a relief. I was

pretty sure I learned enough lessons for one year. For the first time ever, I was feeling like life wasn't so bad in California after all.

With that thought, my phone buzzed in my pocket. It was Jasmin and Keisha.

"Hello, I have so much to tell you both!" I said.

I had to double-check the name of who had called me because for some reason I was face-to-face with a pair of giant green eyes on the screen that were definitely not human.

"You did it!" Keisha's muffled voice was coming from behind the fur of the fluffiest cat I had ever seen. It looked like a dust bunny with eyes.

Since when did she have a cat?

"You helped us find Eloise!" Jasmin and Keisha cheered. They had finally put down the cat and were now sharing the screen, their cheeks smushed together. "Your uncles helped us out big-time."

"Wait, you found her?" I asked.

"Your uncles arrived at my house this morning. They said they found her in some random town a few miles away I'd never heard of. She must have wandered out and gotten lost," Keisha said while petting the cat.

"When did you get a cat?" I asked.

"Eloise *is* a cat." Jasmin rolled her eyes. "You were just looking at her. Who did you think we were talking about this entire time?"

"Ohhhh," I felt ridiculous. "That's Eloise?"

I couldn't believe I didn't realize it sooner. The noise, the chaos, the ruining of their homework. Eloise was a cat. Not a person replacing me as their new best friend.

"Of course she's a cat. What else would she be?" Keisha shoved Eloise's face back into the camera lens so one large green eye filled the frame. She was pretty cute. "My parents got her for me the day you left for California to try to make me less sad about you moving."

"I may have thought Eloise was your new best friend that you were replacing me with." I couldn't believe I had been jealous of a cat.

"We could never replace you," Jasmin said. "Well, at least not *that* quickly."

She laughed and I knew she was joking.

"So every time we told you that Eloise was being a destructive force of nature, you thought she was a person?" Keisha laughed so hard she was practically in tears, and these were definitely the happy kind. Eloise's eyes looked like they were about to pop out of her head from being hugged too tightly.

"I hope you know that we are never letting you live this down," Jasmin said. Her hair was now a bright shade of green for the holidays.

"I'd be shocked if you did." It felt nice to have an inside joke with them again. Even if I'd thought a cat was a person for three months.

"Hey, I've actually got to go." I could smell that my dad was cooking ropa vieja, my favorite, and not the burned kind that Mom makes. "I think it's almost time for dinner and I want to make sure I get to the good stuff before Magdalena devours it all."

"Don't forget to thank your uncles for us!" Keisha flashed Eloise in front of the camera one last time. "You're a real life saver!"

25

A California Christmas

Our first Christmas in LA came sooner than I had expected. I was kind of sad that I wouldn't be spending time with all my family back in Miami, having a big dinner and then opening up presents the night before on Noche Buena. But I had to say, California was finally starting to feel like home.

Mom always liked to go super old-school with her decorating, so the house was decked out in vintage pink tinsel and matching fake trees. Everything in our house was pretty much either pink, white, or chrome and if it weren't for the string lights everywhere, there would definitely be a serious Valentine's Day vibe happening.

"You know you're standing under the mistletoe, right?" I waggled my eyebrows up and down at Beryl and Harrison, who immediately floated in opposite directions.

The warm California air wrapped around my body like a satin blanket as we went outside to admire our lawn, which was covered in flamingo statues wearing Santa hats. Even though I missed the rest of our family back home, I was looking forward to a nice cozy night at home watching reruns of the Christmas episodes of *Everybody's Cousin* as well as seeing my actual cousins on the holiday episode of *Fake It til You Bake It* where apparently Dania actually won! Aunt Rosa may have already tipped us off despite it not having aired yet. I was so proud of her. I even got Mom to admit that the show wasn't the worst. We ended up binge-watching the whole season in a day.

Once Dad finished readjusting a set of lights along the edge of the roof that had gone out, I heard a series of beeping horns behind me. When I turned around, I immediately burst into tears of joy at the sight of my entire family pulling up in front of the house. Each of my aunts, uncles, and cousins was here!

Dad came down from the roof the second he saw the lineup of cars.

"What is this?" I was in total shock.

"It's my Christmas gift to you girls," Mom said. "It wouldn't be the holidays without the family around."

I hugged her as tight as possible and then ran over to help my relatives with their luggage.

"Great job with the lights there." Uncle Raul walked up to Dad and gave him a hearty pat on the back.

Uncle Raul and Uncle Julian were looking extra tan from all their time outdoors looking for lost pets. They had even started their own private business as pet detectives!

"Thank you again for helping my friends find Eloise," I said.

"Any time, kiddo," Uncle Raul said as Uncle Julian tousled my hair.

"Your friends already thanked us on the car ride over." Uncle Julian nodded toward the parade of cars.

"They're here?" I looked out front and saw Jasmin and Keisha, along with their families, waving from their SUV.

"Told you we were planning on visiting!" Jasmin yelled as she was unsuccessfully trying to wrestle Eloise back into her crate.

"I can't believe you came!" My heart felt like it grew three times in size. Is this what the Grinch felt like?

"Where's Abuela?" I asked, noting her absence.

I turned my head in every direction possible to see if she was about to come out of one of the other cars, but she wasn't anywhere to be seen. Abuelito was already here, so why wasn't she with him? He was over by the house helping Dad readjust the lights.

"Don't worry, she's on her way. She had to take a separate car," Keisha said as she started a giant group hug. "I think she mentioned something about wanting better air conditioning so she didn't want to carpool with anybody."

She did always like to make a grand entrance. Ever the performer.

After a few minutes of catching up with my friends and greeting the rest of my family members, the car we had all been waiting for arrived in the driveway. Abuela's driver shivered as he hurried to open the passenger door for her.

I could see that Abuela wasn't alone—she had traveled with an entourage of all of our household ghosts from Miami!

We all crowded inside the house and enjoyed an evening full of laughter and cheer and stories of Abuela's adventures on tour. She even said she would take Magdalena and me with her next year, which Mom actually okayed! I guess sharing the spotlight with Magdalena wouldn't be so bad. We did make a pretty good team.

"Paloma, I want you to know how proud I am of you," Abuela said after she pulled me aside. "You have learned so much in the short amount of time since getting your gift. Your progress impresses me every day. Make sure that you use your abilities in a way that makes yourself proud because I am already proud of you, my darling. Next year will be my best tour yet with you and your sister by my side."

Abuela gave me a giant kiss on the forehead. I could feel the stickiness of her purple lipstick smudge against my skin. I rubbed it off with my shirt sleeve once she started to walk toward the house.

Not too long ago, I would have protested the idea of sharing the stage with Magdalena, but I was looking forward to the three of us traveling together and taking this psychic show on the road.

"I love you, Abuela," I said, taking her hand.

"I love you too, mi amorita." She winked.

I was smiling on the inside and out.

For the rest of the night, my aunts and uncles made predictions like they always did of what was going to happen in the New Year. Even Mom was starting to use her powers again, which everyone was really excited about. But I knew that whatever life had to throw at me, I was ready for it. I was totally psychic after all.

This was truly the best Christmas Eve ever.

★ ★ ★ ★ ★

Acknowledgments

To every single person who believed in me and believed in this book, I want to say my sincerest thank-you.

To the spirits of my loved ones that helped me in my writing process: Grandpa Bill McLaughlin, Abuelita Celia Bajo Gallego, Grandpa "Rochi" Rogelio Gallego, Juan Mato, Hector and Renee Bujia, Grandma Loretta, and Grandpa Jim Martin. Thank you always.

To my family: thank you for being my first readers and for the emotional support along the way. Your wacky personalities and epic yarns are the heart and soul of this novel.

To my parents, Maura and James Martin, for sharing

their faith and sense of wonder. From the fairy footprints we discovered in the foyer to the Elf on the Shelf, thank you for making magic a mainstay in our home.

To my sister, Keara, who always has a prank up her sleeve.

To Peter, Percy, and Walter D'Erasmo for your endless support.

To my friends: I am thankful to every single one of you who listened to my ghost stories and cheered me on.

To my amazing writing mentor, Monica Brown, who is one of the most prolific authors I know.

To the entire amazing teams at Inkyard and Cake. Without the incredible efforts of Claire Stetzer, Shelly Romero, Annie Nybo, Sophia Ramos, Clay Morrell, and Suzie Townsend, I would never have been able to introduce the world to *Totally Psychic*.

To the inimitable Dhonielle Clayton, for her extraordinary vision, creativity, leadership, and kindness.

To every person who touched this book: the production team, the sales team, the designers, the marketing and publicity teams, operations and finance, the warehouse employees, the buyers, the booksellers—I want to thank you all. It takes a lot of hands to bring a book into the world, and I am grateful to every single one of you who helped *Totally Psychic* on its journey.

And finally, to my muse, my wonderful and amazing grandmother Lupe, for always telling me like it is!